"Is the idea of being married to me that repugnant?"

Cole asked.

Darci hesitated just long enough to give his ego a battering. "No."

He fought down irritation that she hadn't jumped at the chance. "You said you were unattached. We can make it a marriage in name only if you'd prefer." The statement cost him every ounce of chivalry he possessed. He longed to have her in his arms.

"I want a family, Cole. I don't want just an empty shell of a marriage, and I don't want to waste my time on a temporary arrangement."

Family. The word pierced Cole's conscience as cleanly as a well-honed knife. Little did Darci know the real reason he was marrying her....

Dear Reader,

What happens when six brides and six grooms wed for *convenient* reasons? Well… In Donna Clayton's *Daddy Down the Aisle,* a confirmed bachelor becomes a FABULOUS FATHER—with the love of an adorable toddler…and his beautiful bride.

One night of passion leaves a (usually) prim woman expecting a BUNDLE OF JOY! In Sandra Steffen's *For Better, For Baby,* the mom-to-be marries the dad-to-be—and now they have nine months to fall in love.…

From secretarial pool to wife of the handsome boss! Well, for a while. In Alaina Hawthorne's *Make-Believe Bride,* she hopes to be his Mrs. Forever—after all, that's how long she's loved him!

What's a rancher to do when his ex-wife turns up on his doorstep with amnesia and a big, juicy kiss? In Val Whisenand's *Temporary Husband,* he simply "forgets" to remind her that they're divorced.…

Disguised as lovey-dovey newlyweds on a honeymoon at the Triple Fork Ranch, not-so-loving police partners uncover their own wedded bliss in Laura Anthony's *Undercover Honeymoon.*…

In debut author Cathy Forsythe's *The Marriage Contract,* a sexy cowboy proposes a marriage of convenience, but when his bride discovers the real reason he said "I do"— watch out!

I hope you enjoy all six of our wonderful CONVENIENTLY WED titles this month—and all of the Silhouette Romance novels to come!

Regards,

Melissa Senate
Senior Editor

Please address questions and book requests to:
Silhouette Reader Service
U.S.: 3010 Walden Ave., P.O. Box 1325, Buffalo, NY 14269
Canadian: P.O. Box 609, Fort Erie, Ont. L2A 5X3

THE MARRIAGE CONTRACT

Cathy Forsythe

Conveniently
Wed

Silhouette®
R O M A N C E™
Published by Silhouette Books
America's Publisher of Contemporary Romance

To Laura, who never let the rules stand in her way.
Here's to scrambled eggs and chicken noodle soup.

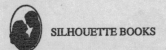 SILHOUETTE BOOKS

ISBN 0-373-19167-7

THE MARRIAGE CONTRACT

Copyright © 1996 by Cathy Forsythe

This edition published by arrangement with Harlequin Books S.A.

® and TM are trademarks of Harlequin Books S.A., used under license. Trademarks indicated with ® are registered in the United States Patent and Trademark Office, the Canadian Trade Marks Office and in other countries.

Printed in U.S.A.

CATHY FORSYTHE

After dealing with the mountains of mud and a zoo full of pets generated by two growing boys, Cathy is ready to settle down to the much cleaner job of writing. With the continued support of her husband, who is hero material himself, she is constantly searching for interesting characters and new story ideas. Now if she can just convince her dog not to be jealous of the computer...

THE MARRIAGE CONTRACT

*With this ring, I thee wed.
I solemnly vow to honor and cherish you
when we are in public and to keep my
hands and desires to myself while in
private. We will join our company stocks,
as we are joining our lives, for the mutual
benefit of Blackmore's Gourmet
Chocolates. We will live together to keep
up the pretense of a happily married
couple. But we will never, ever fall
in love...or will we?*

X *Darci Bradley*

X *Cole Blackmore*

Chapter One

The Denver sky, reflected in the huge glass windows behind her, darkened with gathering thunderclouds, the image matching her worsening mood. A yellow circle of light from her desk lamp offered little comfort as Darci struggled to make the column of numbers work out the way she needed them to. She sighed and scrubbed at her eyes.

It wasn't going to work. They were going to lose it all, and there was nothing she could do to stop it. Mother would never forgive her.

Once more, maybe if she figured it just once more, it would come out right. It had to.

She jumped when a black shadow swished through the air and landed on the desk, scattering her carefully arranged papers. The shadow materialized into a black cowboy hat, and Darci slowly looked up, knowing she wasn't going to like what she saw.

"Little girls shouldn't be out alone after dark."

The warning sent shivers down her spine, just like it had when she *was* a little girl. But the voice was different this time—deeper, harder, almost bitter.

"Cole." Her whisper carried all the confusion, all the pain, all the fears, of these past years. Watching him move closer, she hungrily took in the sight of his lean form.

Her childhood hero had returned. And he still scared the heck out of her.

Cole Blackmore was six feet plus of pure cowboy, radiating the same masculine arrogance he'd claimed even at the age of seventeen—when she'd first met him. Tonight, he wore black, a color that seemed to match the anger emanating from him. Black jeans molded muscular thighs, and a black pearl-buttoned shirt was pulled taut across his broad shoulders. But as usual, a black curl slipped down onto his forehead, spoiling his tough-guy image.

The only relief from the darkness surrounding him was a grim smile barely showing his even, white teeth and a champion-size silver belt buckle that reflected the light from her lamp, causing her to squint slightly.

"You shouldn't be working so late, honey. It'll make you old before your time." He sat in one of the leather chairs across from her and leaned back, his smoky gray eyes carefully watching her for a reaction.

Darci almost smiled. Some things never changed. He'd done the same thing when she was ten years old and he'd just pulled some prank. He always waited, watched to see what she'd do. She'd learned young to bury those reactions and never let him or anyone else see what she was feeling.

She brushed a hand across her blond hair, checking the neatness of the tight chignon she wore to work, trying to buy a few seconds to gather her wits. She hadn't seen Cole in thirteen years, but she'd never quite gotten over that schoolgirl crush. He still made her pulse race and her body temperature rise with little more than a look from his smoldering eyes.

"What are you doing here, Cole? Last I heard, you were in Wyoming, trying to heal another broken bone."

She winced at her words. He didn't need to know that she had followed his career, that she'd saved every newspaper clipping and magazine article since he'd started riding the rodeo circuit. The scrapbook bulged with his successes, and she secretly hoarded her treasure, still dreaming little-girl dreams late at night when she was alone.

He shifted, and she noted the flash of pain that darted across his face. The papers had said it could be a career-ending injury, that the hip joint might never completely heal. She wanted to reach out, needed to comfort him, but knew she'd be flatly rejected.

"I want the company, Darci. I've come to buy out your shares and take over like I was meant to."

The words landed on her ears with the force of a small bombshell. This was *her* company. She'd run it for the past two years, without help, without guidance. Now he wanted to just waltz in and take it away? Her jaw tightened as determination flooded through her. She was the one who had worked late, lost sleep and tried to keep things afloat. Alone, with no help and little guidance.

"This is my office, Cole. And if you'll notice, it says president on the door."

"I own as many shares as you do. And I have as much right, if not more, as you to sit in that chair."

The glittering anger in his eyes should have warned her, but she was fighting for everything she'd allowed herself to dream of. Standing, she braced her clenched fists on the desk as she leaned forward.

"You've never shown the slightest interest. The only way we even knew you were alive was when the dividend checks came back with your signature on them." She gulped, trying to swallow the emotions roiling through her. "And when your daddy was sick, you made no effort to see him." Her voice dropped to a harsh whisper. "You didn't even come to your own father's funeral."

If he had shown some emotion, even a twinge of regret, she might have found a touch of forgiveness in her soul, but he just sat there. Sat and watched, waiting.

"No. I was never the perfect son. I never claimed to be." The bitter tone in his voice increased. "I gave up trying to please the old man when I turned seventeen." His mouth curled with distaste. "When your mother married my father and you both came into our lives, I could see it was hopeless. He doted on you, a sweet, innocent little girl who wasn't even his flesh and blood. He turned away from his own son."

They glared at each other, too angry to speak, too hurt to continue as the seconds ticked away.

Cole sighed and wiped a hand across his mouth. "Look, I didn't come here to fight. And I sure as hell don't want to relive the past. I'll buy out your shares, give you more than market price. You'll be sitting pretty for the rest of your life. You can be a lady of leisure or whatever you want."

"This is my company, and you're not just going to take it away from me." She was proud of the steely ring in her voice. Fear and anger threatened to overwhelm her, to snatch away her vocal cords. But if she showed any weakness now, he'd strike—and he'd strike hard, without a trace of mercy.

He stood and leaned his hands on the desk, his face just inches from hers. She wanted to pull back, to escape from his magnetic aura, but it was too late. He'd already ensnared her in his web.

When he spoke again, his voice was soft, coaxing, the same voice she'd heard him use to calm a nervous horse. "Join me for dinner and we'll talk. I'm sure we can work something out."

His warm breath brushed across her face, stirring an old but never forgotten longing. "I've already eaten, thank you."

She'd never admit her dinner had consisted of a candy bar she'd dug out of her purse. Wanting time to shore up her armor, she needed some distance from the potent force Cole had become. Now that she knew he was back in town, she'd be ready for him. He'd caught her unaware tonight, when she was tired, hungry and in desperate need of a supporting shoulder. If he didn't leave soon, she'd use his and damn the consequences.

"Well, I haven't. Come with me and just have a cup of coffee if you want. But I need to talk with you." He paused for a long heartbeat. "Please."

That quiet entreaty was her downfall. Cole Blackmore never said please, never asked. Ever since she'd met him he'd given orders and expected them to be obeyed. Immediately.

"I suppose I could have a piece of pie or something." She leaned away, desperate for some air that didn't have his male scent mixed with it. Triumph flashed in his eyes and a smile ticked at one corner of his mouth.

"Much obliged, ma'am." With an unconscious flourish, he settled his hat on his head and waited for her to gather her purse and come around the desk. Taking her hand, he pulled it into the crook of his arm and led the way.

She had expected him to take her to someplace quiet, dark, intimate. Someplace where he could seduce her with his masculine will. But he stepped across the street and led her into a brightly lit deli where the air was rich with the mixed scents of spices and coffee. Her mouth watered, reminding her she had skipped lunch today, too.

As she trailed behind him, he placed an order and paid for it. He carried the tray with two sandwiches and two coffees over to a window table and sat down.

"You must be starving," she said. Carefully, she smoothed her skirt underneath, then sat down.

"I am." He plopped one plate in front of her. "And so are you."

"I said I'd already eaten."

"And you never could tell a lie worth a hoot. Now, eat so we can talk."

She bristled at his high-handed assumptions. She was a grown woman now and certainly didn't need him to take care of her. But her stomach loudly reminded her that it had been neglected for too long and that the food here was excellent. She ate, not because he'd told her to, but because she couldn't resist.

Not a word passed between them during their meal. Cole stared moodily out the window, watching the fading nightlife in downtown Denver. It was already past nine o'clock. Most of the stores had closed, and people were slowly drifting away from the restaurants.

With a sigh, Cole leaned back and brought his coffee cup to his lips. After a fortifying gulp, he returned to the unsettling prospect of studying Darci. She'd grown up into a beautiful young woman, a woman who should be out enjoying life, enjoying her youth and finding a man to make a future with. Instead, she was buried in a lonely corporate office, struggling to save a floundering company.

Her blond hair had an added vein of gold running through the strands, gold that he didn't remember seeing when she was little. The pixie face that had grinned at him through braces and thick glasses had matured into a quiet beauty that stirred him in ways the overpainted groupies around the rodeo circuit had never managed. Her long, skinny arms and legs had filled out, giving her a graceful elegance that made him want to take her to his bed for a night of long, slow loving. The prim little business suit hugging her body only added to his longings.

He pushed his thoughts aside with difficulty, determined to get back to the business that had brought him back to Denver, a town he'd vowed never to return to. He didn't want to be here, didn't want to do this. But his options had suddenly become very limited. And he'd do anything for Mandy, do whatever it took to make her life good.

"Can you please explain why you're working so late on a Sunday night? Shouldn't you be home washing your hair or something?" It had been pure luck to find her working tonight. He'd come to the office out of a restless need and found Darci instead of whatever he had been looking for.

She pushed aside her half-eaten sandwich and twisted her coffee cup around in little circles. "The work has to be done, no matter what night of the week it is."

"Don't you have a staff to do that sort of thing?" He knew so little about the company, so little about her life.

But he was about to change all that. One way or another, he'd get what he wanted. And he didn't care what he had to do to achieve his goals.

For just a brief second, the tension and the exhaustion were reflected on her face. But her jaw tightened and the tiredness was washed away, making him wonder if he'd really seen it. He couldn't feel sorry for her, couldn't allow softer emotions to cloud his quest.

"My staff is very small, overworked and doesn't need to know the financial state of the company down to the last penny."

"Is it that bad?"

Her spine stiffened visibly. "No, it's not. But I need to keep up with things, and we're so busy during the day I can't get it all done until everyone leaves and I have some peace and quiet."

Slowly but surely, he'd drawn out the information he needed. But now he had to know about her personal life. Since plan A hadn't left her falling into his arms in gratitude when he took the company off her overworked hands, he needed to revert to plan B. Other than a loss of his freedom, it would be only a small personal sacrifice to blend his life with Darci's. In fact, it was becoming more enticing with every passing minute.

"There must be a man somewhere who's waiting at home for you to call."

"There's no one."

Her words were clipped short, and he studied her carefully, noting the fresh pain reflected in her eyes. He should be celebrating, because physically she was free for the taking. But emotionally, he suspected she was still attached to someone. He'd just have to proceed as planned. His scheme didn't require her love, just her cooperation.

"You won't consider selling?"

She shook her head adamantly. "It's my company, Cole."

"Actually, it's *our* company." He waited for that assertion to soak in. "We own equal shares and equal rights."

"But the board has appointed me president. I'm in charge until they change their minds."

"That can be arranged, I'm sure." He disliked the quiet threat, but he needed to back her into a corner, needed to force her to turn to him.

Her green eyes glared daggers at him. "Are you threatening me?"

"Just stating facts." He leaned forward, trying to hold her gaze, but her look darted away. "Blackmore's Gourmet Chocolates is my legacy, the only thing I've ever had from the old man." His grip on the coffee cup tightened until his knuckles turned white. "I sure as hell never had his love."

Without warning, her fingers curled around his wrist, offering an understanding he didn't want.

"Your father was a hard man. And you made it very difficult for him to show you anything other than his anger."

The years of arguing, of fighting to be his own man, haunted Cole. His father had never understood Cole's need to make something on his own, to carve his own path. He hadn't wanted just to inherit his father's life and keep up with the image until retirement.

But after years of struggling, of more success in his chosen profession than he'd ever dreamed possible, Cole had no options left. He needed to come home, to take over the family gourmet candy business and make his father proud. Even if it was too late.

"Darci, I intend to take control of the company. Sell your shares and let me have what's rightfully mine."

She pulled away, and he felt a momentary sense of loss. Her warmth had lit a little patch of sunshine in his cold heart. He didn't want to lose it, but knew he had no right to keep it.

"You may be his son by blood, but I was there for him when he needed family." Her voice shook with an unnamed emotion. "Through the endless tests at the hospital, through all the gut-wrenching decisions, through the pain and the finality of his death, I was there. I arranged the funeral, I settled the estate, and now I'm running the family business. Where were you?"

Her words hit him in the gut harder than any fighting calf ever could have. It was all true. She'd earned the right to her position in the company, but he needed it. And he'd never let a little thing like right or wrong stand in his way before. He took what he wanted in any way he had to.

"I was out getting my head busted, trying to make my father proud." *Trying to accomplish the impossible.*

"You may be too late."

He laughed, the sound bitter even to his ears. "I know I'm too late. He's dead. But I have to prove to myself that I could have done it if I'd wanted to."

She shook her head. "That's not what I meant. Uncle John is trying to force me out, trying to throw his percentage of the shares into the battle for control."

"But you own—"

"Only a small percentage by myself. He holds almost as much, and my mother has sided the strength of her shares with him. Without any communication from you for all these years, that gives him a lot of power with the board of directors. And they're starting to lean his way."

She sucked in a deep breath, and he could see the effort it was taking her to remain strong. "Nothing I've tried has worked. I can't seem to find the magic formula to pull the company out of this slump. And with a board meeting next week, I suspect I'm out of time."

"Darci, I—"

"So don't threaten me with failure, Cole. I'm already staring it right in the face." She fell silent, her eyes bright with unshed tears, her lips clenched.

Suddenly, he smiled as a memory washed over him. "And you won't call 'uncle' no matter what, will you? You never did as a child." He laughed, this time feeling delight at the recollection of the little girl who had tried to fix his life for him.

When she returned his smile, there was a touch of wistfulness around the edges. "I was young and stubborn. It's a terrible combination that I'm lucky I survived."

"I wasn't going to let you get hurt that time you followed me up the foothills."

"You could have fooled me."

He'd been seventeen and madder than hell after another fight with his father. Darci had insisted on following him, determined to protect him from himself, to talk to him and try to fix things. Cole had hiked up into the foothills behind their house and proceeded to take the most difficult route to the top. And Darci had stuck with him, tongue clenched between her teeth, puffing hard as she gamely tried to struggle up rock outcroppings taller than she was.

He'd been hoping to lose her, to make her give up, but she'd earned his grudging admiration that day. Before the hike was over, he'd carried her piggyback because she'd twisted her ankle. But he hadn't let her know how much her caring had touched him. He'd just pulled her pigtails until she squealed; then he'd walked away, carrying a tiny piece of warmth in a dark corner of his soul.

Their memories touched, melded and gave them a common bond that had been long forgotten.

A bond he forced himself to ignore as he went after what he needed for his very survival. "You won't sell to me, will you."

"No." The single word carried all the arguments she hadn't spoken.

"Separately, we're weak, almost helpless. Neither one of us has a big enough chunk of stock to stop Uncle John." He leaned back in the chair and tipped his hat back on his head. "I won't sell to you, even if you had the money to buy me out, so where does that leave us?"

"Without a prayer."

He almost smiled in silent victory. He had her right where he wanted her.

"Then let's get married."

Her mouth dropped open, and she stared at him in disbelief. He gently reached out and nudged her chin up with one finger. "You'll catch flies that way."

"I'm sorry, I don't think I heard what you said."

"Marry me. We were each supposed to receive additional stock as a wedding present. That was part of the old man's will. Combining what we have would give us controlling stock. If we work together, maybe we can keep Blackmore's out of John's greedy fingers."

The color washed out of her skin, and she swayed slightly. Cole braced his hand on her shoulder, afraid she was going to crash to the floor.

"Darci?"

She blinked and seemed to focus her eyes on his face.

"There has to be another way."

"Probably, but this will give us the most power within the company. It's the fastest, most efficient way." He waited for several heartbeats, studying her, trying to gauge her reaction—trying to ignore the frustration building inside of him. "Is the idea of being married to me that repugnant?"

She hesitated just long enough to give his ego a battering. "No."

"Would you consider the idea?" He fought down a sense of irritation that she hadn't jumped at the chance. Most of the women he'd known wouldn't have hesitated to accept his offer.

"This is a little fast, Cole."

"You said you were unattached. We can make it a marriage in name only if you'd prefer." The statement cost him every ounce of chivalry he possessed. Since he'd stood in the doorway of her darkened office, watching her work, he'd longed to have her in his arms. But once the marriage was official, he could work on the physical side of it. First, he had to maneuver himself into a position of power, then turn it to his advantage.

"I want a family, Cole. I don't want just an empty shell of a marriage, and I don't want to waste my time on a temporary arrangement."

Family. The word pierced Cole's conscience as cleanly as a well-honed knife. Little did Darci know the real reason he was marrying her. "But first, you have to gain control of the company or you'll lose everything."

She remained silent, the truth of his words reflected in her eyes.

"It's the only way we can both have what we want."

"Will I still be president, or will you take that over, too?"

"You can be president and I'll be vice president in charge of something or other. But we'll work together, make the decisions together and take control together."

"But what about—"

"Darci, do you want my help? Do you want to keep this company under your leadership?" He was playing dirty, pushing her to make a decision before she had time to think, but he didn't have any choice. His situation had turned desperate, all other options had been ripped from his hold.

"Yes."

"For now, let's agree on a one-year marriage. We'll work out the other details later. Our first concern is getting the corporation back on solid ground. We need to move quickly or we stand to lose everything."

Slowly, the color returned to her face and he risked releasing his hold on her. He held out his hand across the table.

"Deal, partner?"

She hesitated, running her tongue across her lips and leaving a tantalizing trail of wetness. Slowly, she lifted her hand and placed it in his.

The softness of her skin sent a charge racing up his arm that almost made him pull back. The desire he held for her would be very dangerous. But he'd courted danger before and won. He could do it again.

"Deal. When do we make it official?"

He suppressed his sigh of relief. He'd gotten what he wanted with very few concessions on his part. Now he was in a position to manipulate the future to fit his needs, to do what he needed to help Mandy. "I'll meet with my lawyer in the morning and have the papers drawn up. You can have your lawyer look them over, and if we all agree, we'll do the deed. The sooner we move, the better, because we need to present a united front at that meeting next week.''

He stood and settled his hat so it again shaded his eyes. Someday, he'd have to tell her more about why he needed to marry her, about why he needed to work at a job he'd vowed never to hold. Someday soon. Tipping her chin up with his knuckles, he stared into her eyes, trying to gauge her reactions to all that had happened in the past few hours. But she was almost as good as he was at concealing what she felt. All he could identify was a deep wariness.

Of him.

He nodded and walked away without looking back. Good. If she was wary of him, that gave him a weakness to use to his advantage. And he'd need every advantage he could find if he was going to pull this off. For the first time in years, he had a plan, a goal. And for the first time in years, he felt truly alive again, ready for the next battle.

The quiet of the night slipped around him as he stepped outside, reassuring him he was doing the right thing. His pride had taken a beating these last few months. But he was about to change all that, about to grab his future and direct his destiny again. He caught one more tantalizing glimpse of Darci in the window before turning away.

Darci sat stone still, watching Cole's reflection in the plate-glass window until he disappeared from sight. Only then did she allow her head to drop into her hands, showing the first sign of weakness since he'd walked back into her life.

Little girls' dreams rarely came true, and hers had suddenly turned into a shadowed nightmare.

Excitement and dread warred for her attention. The attraction she felt for Cole was stronger than ever, had built on her childhood fantasies and become a force to be respected. Suddenly, she was going to have to face him every day, every night, and not let him see how much he affected her.

Playing with fire had always held an appeal to her, but she'd never indulged herself before. Danger and excitement in her life were things she'd silently craved but never had the courage to pursue. Without thinking through the consequences, she'd just promised to leap into the flames and dance with the most dangerous man she'd ever met—a man who held the power to destroy her in more ways than one.

A tingle of exhilaration washed through her. Heaven help her, but she'd just made a date with the devil himself.

Chapter Two

Her hand trembled as she tried to smooth on the muted tones of eye shadow. She clenched her fingers tighter around the small brush and tried again. The effect was a little off, but no one would notice. They'd be too busy looking at the smudged shadows under her eyes.

The night had passed in an agony of self-doubt, of second-guessing the decision she'd made so quickly.

Married.

At one time, marrying Cole had been her childhood fantasy. She'd loved the younger version of Cole with all the intensity that only a ten-year-old could muster. And that puppy love still lingered, making her wish for more.

She wanted to reach out to Cole and hang on for the rest of her life. But she forced herself to remember his offer was little more than a fantasy that would disappear at the end of one year. The reality was he only wanted to marry her for her shares of stock. Just like Jeffrey.

There hadn't been a trace of love in Cole's tense posture, in his watchful look while he waited for her answer. Wariness, hope, maybe even a touch of desperation, but no love, no desire, nothing that would make their marriage anything more than a cold, calculated business deal.

He'd eventually leave her. After all, everyone she'd ever deeply loved had left her. First her natural father had walked away from his family without warning then her step-father had died. Even when Cole had left that first time, Darci's young heart had taken it as a form of desertion. And he was going to leave her again. But this time, she'd know it was coming. This time, she'd be prepared.

This time, she wouldn't be hurt.

She squeezed her eyes closed on the pain that pierced her heart. Was it asking so much to be loved, to be needed by someone? To have them stand by her side no matter what?

So far, her father's company had been the only constant in her life, the only thing that hadn't deserted her. It was her family right now, her security. But now that was about to be ripped away from her, too.

The dream of home and family still lingered, long beyond her disillusionment with the possibility of such a life. She wanted children, a family, a loving home to nurture and care for. She couldn't totally give up hope, couldn't believe that it wasn't still in the future for her. Cole just wasn't the man to provide what she wanted. He was simply a means to save the company. She'd do well to remind herself of that loud and often. It was the only protection she had right now.

She tugged at the tailored suit jacket, knowing she looked good, looked professional. But she couldn't help wishing that her appearance was a bit more feminine, a touch more alluring. For Cole.

When she walked into the outer offices of Blackmore's Gourmet Chocolates, she kept her sunglasses on until she reached the sanctuary of her own office. With a sigh of relief, she slipped the glasses off and tucked them into her purse. When her secretary, Alex, came in, he stopped and stared at her.

"You look terrible."

"Thank you, that's just what I needed to hear." She smiled to soften her words, then held out her hand for the messages he held. At first, she'd felt awkward with a male secretary, but soon found he was efficient and dedicated to her needs, just as he'd been for her mentor, Cole's father.

Alex crossed the room to pull open the curtains now blocking the view of the Colorado Rockies. "Good party?"

"No party, I just had a lot on my mind last night and couldn't sleep."

Alex immediately returned to business. They had a friendly relationship, but had always made an effort to keep everything on a professional keel. He listed her meetings for the day, waited for instructions, then disappeared, closing her door softly behind him.

Darci leaned back in her chair and sighed. She'd never make it through the day. A dull headache pounded at the base of her neck, and her eyes felt gritty.

Raised voices intruded on her moment of peace, and she lifted her head just in time to watch her door burst open and Cole stride through, Alex following closely behind.

"You can't go in there without an appointment."

"I can do anything I want. And I can see my wife anytime I want."

Alex halted just outside the doorway, his surprised gaze darting back and forth between Darci and Cole. Cole gave the door a shove and it slammed in Alex's face.

Darci debated between groaning or screaming, but finally decided neither would register with Cole. He'd never made things easy for her, why should he start now?

"That little twerp isn't really your secretary, is he?"

"Good morning, Cole. How are you today?" She struggled to control her temper, knowing she needed Cole more than he needed her right now. And shouting at him for his bad manners wouldn't have any more effect on him than it had when he was seventeen.

Cole stopped halfway across the room and cocked his head, his black cowboy hat shading his eyes from her view. It didn't matter, because she probably wouldn't be able to tell what was clicking through his mind, anyway. But just once, she'd like to have the ability to read him, to know what he was thinking, without having to rely on words that didn't always tell the truth.

A smile broke over his lips, and she fought the urge to think anything was possible with him by her side. "I'm fine, thank you, ma'am. And you?"

"Terrible." She pulled a stack of papers in front of her and grabbed a pen. "Please try to treat my staff with respect from now on. It wouldn't have hurt you to wait until Alex called me before you came in."

"I'm not used to being put on hold, for anyone or anything. But I'll work on it."

His concession was too easy, but she decided not to press him lest she come out the loser. "And we're not married yet, so please refrain from calling me your wife until we are."

"Just practicing."

She knew that was as close as she would get to an apology, so she decided to drop the subject. There were too many other things on her mind right now. Like how good Cole looked in the dark blue shirt he wore today, how his jeans fit him to perfection, how his deep, drawling voice trickled over her skin like warm sand...

Her intercom buzzed, and she picked up the receiver. A tired smile pulled at her lips when she heard Alex's voice ask if she was all right.

"Yes, Alex. Everything is in order. I'll explain the circumstances to you as soon as...Cole leaves. Hold all my calls, will you?"

"Protective, isn't he?" Cole settled himself in one of the leather chairs across from her desk, propping his hat on one knee.

She massaged her forehead, wondering how many aspirin she dared take at once. "If I yelled, screamed and kicked my feet, would you go away?"

A grin touched one corner of his mouth. "Probably not."

"Then I'll tell you this only once. Alex is a very loyal, hard-working employee who has stood by me no matter what. If you can't treat him with respect, don't bother coming back here."

One black eyebrow rose at her words. "You've grown up, honey. Have you tested those claws on anyone yet or do men fall for all that angry bluster?"

"Cole, I'm tired. I'm angry. I'm frustrated. And I feel like I've been backed into a corner." She slammed her pencil down on the desk. "Don't push me too hard right now or you just might find out how hard I can push back.''

Cole wisely chose to remain silent.

After several seconds ticked past, Darci nodded her head, accepting his silent agreement. ''Did you need something in particular?''

He placed a sheaf of papers on her desk. ''You need to take this to your lawyer, then sign it.''

Darci glanced at the first page and felt a wave of cold dread sweep over her. The contract that would define their lives as husband and wife. It was all written out neatly in black and white with plenty of legalese.

''Basically, we're agreeing to equal shares and equal control in the business, unless the board changes our positions. All personal assets will remain the sole property of the current owner and there will be no settlements owed by either party when we choose to end the marriage.''

Darci forced herself to speak through cold lips. ''In other words, after our divorce, everything returns to the way it was and it's like the marriage never happened.''

He nodded. ''It sounds like you've got it all neat and tidy.'' She clutched the papers tightly, a wealth of emotions churning through her. ''I'll have my lawyer look it over and get back with you tomorrow afternoon.''

''We don't have that much time, Darci.''

She raised her gaze to meet his, silently waiting for him to continue.

''The wedding is scheduled for five o'clock tonight at the courthouse. You'll need to have the papers completed by then.'' He paused, then continued as if his words hadn't almost stopped her heartbeat. ''Do you want me to pick you up or should we meet there?''

"The—" An unsettling combination of fear and desire coursed through her. She cleared her throat and tried to focus her thoughts on what he'd just announced. "Don't you think that's a little fast?"

His mouth flattened into a grim line. "One thing we have very little of is time. This is Monday, that will give us a few days to get acquainted, set a game plan and be ready for the meeting next Monday." He studied her intently. "And it's the only time the judge is available this week."

She pulled a slow, calming breath into her lungs, trying to force her mind to come up with an argument. She needed time to think, time to work through all the pitfalls of the step they were about to take. But Cole was acting like the world would end if they didn't get married fast.

And maybe it would. At least her world, the world she'd built around the company, the only world she knew or wanted.

"I'll call my lawyer right away." She swallowed the sigh hovering on her lips. "What will you be wearing?"

His grin stretched across his face. "I thought I could at least dress up for my own wedding. I have one suit that's respectable, and I'll even polish my boots for you. We can pick out rings tomorrow, and then I can move my gear in with you."

"Is it necessary for us to live together?"

Cole watched her, stalked her with his will. "The board is more likely to go along with us if they believe we're married for all eternity. A marriage of convenience doesn't always last that long, does it?"

"It will be a big adjustment for me. I've lived alone for several years now." And suddenly she'd be expected to share her life with a very potent, very virile, very tempting man.

"We'll work out the details later, honey. For now, let's just get through the formalities."

A warm flush washed over her as intimate scenes of the two of them living together flashed through her thoughts. She lived in a two-bedroom condo with a magnificent view of the Rocky Mountains. But it was a small space and it would shrink even more once Cole settled his disturbing aura into her space.

And she only had one bed. One very big, very lonely bed. One bed that she would never consent to sharing with a husband who wanted her only for her portion of the company stock.

She forced her thoughts away from the tantalizing idea of spending the night in Cole's arms and glanced down at her own clothing. "I guess I'd better make a quick shopping trip over lunch and find something suitable."

When she looked up again, he was leaning close. "Anything you wear will be perfect as far as I'm concerned."

His heated gaze drifted over the upper half of her body, and suddenly she felt thoroughly loved. Her heart squeezed out a single tear of longing.

If only it were true, if only she could be looking forward to this wedding as the culmination of a proper courtship, something that would be the final seal on a deep, lasting love. If only she could be sharing her dreams of a family with this man. If only she could still believe in fairy tales.

She briskly shuffled the papers on her desk. "I'll try to find something appropriate." Glancing at her watch, she stood. "I have a meeting in a few minutes. Can I do anything else for you?"

The businesslike persona was her only armor right now. If she wasn't careful, he'd break through her defenses and find out just how much she wanted him—to love her, to need her, to want her.

A grim smile touched her lips. Little girls didn't always manage to grow out of their fantasies.

Her carefully constructed defenses shattered when he leaned across the desk and touched his lips to hers. It was little more than a whisper of sensation, but she felt it all the way to the foundations of her soul.

"At least we won't have to change the monogram on the towels. You're simply changing your name from Bradley to Blackmore. Convenient, huh?"

He stepped away as if totally unaffected by the kiss. He pulled out a business card and laid it on her desk. "You need to stop at this clinic before lunch for the blood test. They promised to have the results for me to pick up on the way to the courthouse."

She stared at the card, not reaching out to touch it.

Cole turned to leave. Hesitating with his hand on the doorknob, he stared at her. "You will be there, won't you?" For the first time, his own doubts and fears peeked through the tough cowboy veneer.

"I said I would. We both know why we're doing this and that it has to be done. Don't worry, I won't be late for my own wedding."

He tipped his hat and left the room without another word.

Darci sat very still, staring vaguely at the closed door. She was in big trouble. Because she was far from immune to Cole's special brand of cowboy charm. In fact, she suspected she could become very addicted to it. And that meant she was setting herself up for another heartbreak. One she just might not survive.

Darci sent Alex to her lawyer's office with the contract and a note saying she needed an immediate response, then she tried to forget about it and get back to work.

But she was so distracted during the meeting with her personnel manager she was finally forced to delay the discussion for another day. When she returned to her office, she asked Alex to cancel any other appointments, claiming a headache.

"Darci?"

She stopped just before going into her office and turned. Alex stood and moved toward her uncertainly.

"I know we've always made it a point to keep our relationship strictly professional, but I can't help but worry about you. Is everything all right?"

She had the urge to laugh, but knew it would have a hysterical edge to it. "Everything is as all right as it can be, Alex. Thank you for caring."

"The man who was here this morning, your husband, does he have free access to your office?"

Darci squeezed her eyes closed, trying to hide from what needed to be said. "He's not my husband until five o'clock this afternoon, Alex. And yes, he's to have free access to my office."

She started to open the door, then paused. "Would you make certain Mr. Jamison's old office is cleaned tonight? Mr. Blackmore will be taking over that space soon. And see what you can do about finding a secretary for him within our own staff, would you?"

"Mr. Blackmore?"

She smiled awkwardly. "It's a long story, Alex. In as few words as possible, I'm marrying my step-brother in a last-ditch effort to save this company from total ruin." With a frantic twist of the handle, the door popped open and she fell through it gratefully. Alex's shocked expression would stay with her for the rest of the afternoon. His was only the first reaction she would have to get beyond. There were many more people who would be even more stunned by her sudden marriage.

She'd almost made it to her desk when she realized just what she'd said to her secretary. Darting back through the door, she stopped him before he reached the hallway. "Alex." She halted, not knowing how to say what needed to be said. "What I just told you, that's in the strictest confidence."

Alex only nodded. "As is everything we discuss in this office, Darci. If you're certain this is what needs to be done, I'll support you in every way that I can. And I can see the necessity of casting an illusion of lasting love on your pending relationship." He turned away. "If you need nothing further, I'll see to that office now."

"Thank you, Alex." His perception of the needs of any situation had always made Alex invaluable. When the company could see daylight again, she'd have to see about getting him a raise. A big one.

She massaged the bridge of her nose, trying to relieve her mounting stress. There was at least one phone call that needed to be made before she went shopping. Mother should be warned that Cole was back in town. Maybe Darci would omit the news of their marriage until at least their first wedding anniversary. If they made it that far.

Darci swung her desk chair around to stare out the window. The afternoon sun glinted off the nearby buildings, adding a glow that the downtown area often lacked. The tall buildings tended to shadow one another, leaving the area with a sense of gloom that was difficult to shake.

Darci's mother and Cole had disliked each other from the first moment they met. Cole had been a rebellious teenager, ready and willing to go against anything that was expected of him. Father and son had set a pattern of disagreeing over everything for years before the new family had moved in, and nothing had changed with the addition of two females to the household.

The new Mrs. Blackmore had tried to lay down rules Cole had no intention of obeying, and then the fights had begun in earnest. Daddy had tried to stop them, but had only succeeded in further alienating Cole from the fractured family.

And Darci had just wanted them all to love one another. She'd run frantically from person to person, making excuses, trying to patch things up, desperately needing a happy family to call her own. But no matter how hard she had tried, how many times she had made excuses for one of them, it had all fallen apart about six months later. Cole had packed his bags, leaving the house for the final time. Mrs. Anita Blackmore had been there to wish him good riddance.

Now the past had returned to haunt Darci. She knew she'd once again be thrown into the position of peace-keeper. She just wasn't certain her heart was in it this time. The temptation was to let them hate each other, to just keep them apart. But there was still that little girl that so desperately wanted a real family—a family that would laugh together, play together and love one another no matter what.

Another childhood fantasy that didn't stand a fair chance of coming true.

The ringing of the phone pulled Darci from her thoughts, and she gratefully reached for the distraction. But when Alex put her lawyer through, she wished she'd been elsewhere. As important as that contract was, she wanted to act like it didn't exist, like there might be a chance for the marriage to become something lasting.

After a few cryptic questions, James Wells agreed that everything was legal and wouldn't endanger her personal assets in any way. But after the business was taken care of, there was a long pause that made Darci consider hanging up to avoid the question hovering between them.

"Is there any other way, Darci?"

She closed her eyes, knowing he understood more than most people would. He'd been the family attorney for more than twenty years and knew the condition of the business. "If there is, I can't see it right now, James."

"Well, good luck to you, then. And call me if there's anything I can do. Anything, Darci."

She agreed and slowly replaced the receiver.

After a slight hesitation, she decided to get all the unpleasantness out of the way at once and dialed her mother's number. Darci knew she'd have to take charge of the conversation to avoid unwanted questions about business. Questions that had no answers and few solutions.

At her mother's hello, Darci threw out the bait. "Cole's back in Denver."

There was a beat of silence. "Why?"

"He wants Blackmore's. Offered to buy me out."

"It figures. He must have finally partied away all that money he's made over the years. Now he wants to dip into ours, but I'm sure he doesn't intend to work for it."

Darci's heartbeat accelerated as she prepared to say the words she knew would cause an explosion. "Cole and I have decided to get married."

Total silence greeted her words.

"We'll be at the board meeting together, and I plan to appoint Cole as vice president." Still no words crossed the telephone wires. "I just thought you would like to know." Darci desperately wanted a response, any response. Deep down, she longed to hear the words of a mother wanting her daughter's happiness. But Anita Blackmore had never considered that in the past.

The unspoken truth hovered between them, the fact that this wasn't a union of love, but a business arrangement.

"When?"

The single word held a wealth of meaning. And Darci heard each argument, every criticism, through the silence.

"Five o'clock this afternoon, at the courthouse."

A click sounded in her ear and Darci stared at the phone, knowing she shouldn't let her mother hurt her, knowing Anita couldn't change even if she would ever admit she was wrong.

Determined to escape the past, along with her own doubts, Darci grabbed her purse. The business, her mother and rest of the world would simply have to get along without her for a while. It was her wedding day, and even though she didn't feel the glow of nervous anticipation most brides experienced, she was determined to expend a little effort to make it special.

A quick trip to the health clinic made what she was about to do suddenly very real. And it made her wish she had the option of calling everything off.

She wandered the sidewalk for long minutes after the blood test, trying to work up the courage to buy herself a wedding dress. Finally, she forced herself to turn into

a large department store where she could hope for ano-
nymity. On display was a simple cream-colored silk dress
with flowing lines that reminded her of angels and forgotten dreams.

Darci bought it on impulse after seeing the way it
hugged her body. She might not be expecting a true
wedding night, but she could at least tempt him a little
bit. Maybe just enough to get him to kiss her like he really meant it.

Finishing her outfit off with matching shoes and gold
jewelry took only a few minutes. Darci stopped long
enough to hover over the wedding rings in the display
case, then forced herself to turn away. That was a sym-
bol of love and commitment she wasn't certain she was
ready for.

Their marriage was little more than a business arrangement. Those words mocked her as she forced herself to view her future as Cole's wife, a future that lacked
the deep, abiding love she craved.

She quickly changed clothes at her office, trying to
silence the voices arguing in her head. Every shred of her
being warned her she was setting herself up for a big
hurt, that she wanted Cole too badly to keep any distance between them. But the alternatives could destroy
her when the end came.

After signing the contract with her lawyer as a wit-
ness, Darci left for the courthouse in a haze of confusion. She wanted so much more from her marriage, but
then had to remind herself this one might only last a few
years. Once the company was solid again, Cole would no
doubt want a divorce so he could get on with his life.

They could still split the business duties without actually sharing their lives.

By the time she found a parking space, she'd managed to convince herself her marriage to Cole was little different than signing an employment contract. As she walked into the courthouse, she buried her softer needs in a dark, cold corner of her heart, saving them for the day when she married for love. Feeling safe and confident that she could handle being Cole's wife, she opened the door to the judge's outer office.

When she spotted Cole on the other side of the room, all her confidence crumbled into little more than dust at her feet.

His charcoal western suit fit him to perfection, reminding her that his shoulders were broad enough to help carry her problems. A gray cowboy hat rested on the desk beside him, waiting once again to shade his emotions from the world.

His gray eyes gleaming, he stepped forward with a fragrant bouquet of white roses and gently placed the flowers in her cold fingers. "I thought the bride should at least have flowers," he said quietly. Pulling out a single blossom, he tucked it into her blond hair, a soft smile of satisfaction on his lips. "I was hoping you'd wear it down so I could see how long it was."

Darci stared at him, recognizing the gleam of possessiveness in his eyes and wondering at the source. Then she reminded herself that he was gaining control of Blackmore's Gourmet Chocolates in this deal. With a sinking heart, she acknowledged the possessiveness wasn't for her, but for the bottom line of what he considered his heritage.

The judge stepped into the room, and suddenly all the doubts overwhelmed Darci. Trying to keep her terror from showing in her eyes, she turned to the man standing calmly by her side. "Cole, I—"

"It's all right, honey." He trailed work-hardened fingers across her cheek. "I'll make it right for both of us."

Her fears settled a little at his reassurance, and she turned to face her wedding vows with a semblance of confidence. The judge spoke the words that would bind them together, first getting Cole's agreement to the marriage, then waiting for Darci to answer. Before she could open her mouth, there was a commotion in the hallway.

"Darci, I refuse to allow this madness." Her mother sailed into the room with all the regal splendor of the Queen Mother. Turning to the judge, she said, "These two don't love each other and shouldn't be allowed to marry."

Cole's lips tightened. "Is there a law that says we have to prove our love before the wedding ceremony?"

The judge peered over his glasses at the family drama playing out before him, his expression not changing. "Love is not required, but I like to see some sense of commitment before I bind two people together."

Cole looked down at Darci, and she felt the force of his determination reaching out to her, demanding her support. "We're committed, I can promise you that. Aren't we, Darci?"

She nodded, more than willing to let him fight this particular battle. Her reserves of strength had been used up hours ago, and now she just wanted to lean on the strong man at her side. Just long enough to recover, to regroup.

"Darci, I refuse to allow you to do this."

Darci was finally forced to face her mother. Pushed to fight a battle that should have been fought years ago, she spoke the words that needed to be said. "I'm over twenty-one, Mother. You have no say in the matter."

"Then I'll no longer consider you my daughter. You and that man will not be welcome in my home." The woman waited silently, certain her daughter would give in and walk away from Cole.

The betrayal knifed through Darci as she turned her back on her only living blood relative. Placing her hand in Cole's, she calmly voiced her agreement to the marriage, ignoring the tears stinging at her eyes. Cut adrift in a sea of emotions, she turned to lift her face to her husband for the traditional kiss.

He leaned closer. Just before his mouth touched hers, he murmured, "And the show begins."

His lips touched her cheek, then slid to her mouth, and she forgot all about right and wrong, obligation and commitment. This was her husband and she wanted him. They had a budding friendship between them, a common goal, and maybe the rest would come with time and patience.

Tentatively, she touched her tongue to his lips. With a low groan, he wrapped his arms around her and pulled her closer, staking his new ownership thoroughly and completely.

His warmth enfolded her, threatened to consume her, as their tongues met for the first time.

And all her childhood fantasies paled in the face of reality.

Darci suddenly knew she was in very deep water without a hope of swimming to safety. She wanted Cole with all her being, but didn't know how to ask for him. But most of all, she wanted to be loved, cherished and needed. She wanted to build a family with Cole and make a happy home.

She wanted the impossible.

Chapter Three

The whiskey burned a trail down his throat and settled in his stomach, joining another heat that wouldn't be assuaged by anything other than a long, hot night of loving his new wife. Cole stared out his hotel room window into the darkness, wondering just how badly he'd managed to screw things up this time.

Guilt gnawed at the edges of his thoughts. He'd run roughshod over Darci, had forced her to make decisions without time to think of the consequences. He'd bullied her into agreeing to what he wanted, then walked away.

And he hadn't told her about Mandy.

Now he wasn't certain he could handle the reins of the new life he'd mapped out for them.

Memories of their wedding day drifted through his mind—the family tensions, his own buried secrets, the trust he'd seen in Darci's eyes as they said their vows. He was going to have to be very, very careful with her. Because there were still remnants of that lost little girl lingering in her eyes. And that little girl could still get to places he'd thought he'd locked away forever.

The innocent eagerness that colored everything Darci did, her beauty... her response to his kiss. All three would haunt him for a long time. But he had to remember he had a job to do. He had to remember he was doing it all for Mandy.

Rolling the glass between his palms, he tried to cool his wayward thoughts. This afternoon, when he'd kissed Darci for the first time as his wife, he'd suddenly found himself wishing it were all for real. But if it were, then he'd be breaking a vow he'd made years ago, a vow that wouldn't allow him to love again. Love in any form was too painful, too consuming. Love ate a man alive, then threw him away without a second thought.

Except for Mandy. Mandy was different. She loved him no matter what he did. All he had to do was love her back—something he'd been terrified he wasn't capable of until he'd looked into her newborn eyes and let her hold his finger. From that moment on, he knew he'd do anything for her.

Including marry a woman who held the power to destroy what little was left of the man Cole had become.

His humorless laugh haunted the room. What would the old man think of his son now? What would he think of the marriage, the motives behind it? Cole could almost hear the angry words, the accusations. The two of them would still disagree, still argue over everything, and probably never find a kind word to say to each other. But Cole couldn't help wishing that, just once, his father had said he was proud of his son.

A knock sounded at the door, interrupting his self-recriminations. Setting his empty glass aside with a sense of relief, he braced himself for what he expected on the other side.

And he wasn't disappointed. Darci stood in the hallway, still wearing her wedding dress. The dark circles under her eyes had deepened, adding to the haunted look she'd carried throughout the day. Cole struggled with the urge to drag her into his arms and soothe her. But she'd misunderstand his offering and he'd be crossing a boundary he wasn't certain he dared approach.

He suspected neither of them had been ready for the intimacy of their first dinner together as a married couple. He'd offered to call room service so they could begin the planning right away, but Darci had insisted she had some business to finish at the office. Cole had accepted her excuse gratefully, needing time to gather his thoughts, to adjust to this new twist in his life.

"Hi." He swept his arm back. "Come in, I'll order drinks and we can talk."

She shook her head, tiny curls of escaping hair dancing around her face. "No. I'd rather we went for a walk or something."

He almost smiled. So she was feeling as awkward as he was. But his awkwardness was a direct result of the unwanted, unexpected, burning desire for his wife. Hers was probably more from a need to keep a sense of distance between them.

He knew she wanted him, could read the desire in her eyes every time she looked at him. And he now had a legal right to take advantage of that desire. But he wasn't ready, couldn't bear the thought of exposing his heart to more pain. Because he knew if he allowed himself to take her, he'd learn to care for her.

Nodding, Cole grabbed his hat and ushered her toward the elevator. But all his vows didn't prevent him from enjoying the gentle sway of her hips as she walked in front of him. The swishing silk covered her slender legs to a point just below the knee, revealing much less than he would have liked. Maybe someday, if fate were finally kind to him, he'd have the privilege of viewing the long length of her bare limbs. For now, he'd have to rely on his imagination, which was working overtime, building memories that hadn't even been created yet.

As they stepped outside, Cole savored the brush of the cool night air against his skin. The evening cleared the cobwebs from his thoughts, but did little to cool his libido. He let Darci walk beside him for a few minutes, then reached out and took her hand in his. She jerked and turned a distrustful gaze on him.

"Relax. It's all part of the show. If you jump every time I touch you, no one will ever believe our charade." Her fingers slowly loosened, then stiffly settled against his hand. The simple gesture sent a flood of heat curling through him again.

"Does it have to be that way? Can't we just act like business associates in the office and stay out of the public eye the rest of the time?"

"Running scared already, little girl?"

She jerked her hand away and folded her arms under her breasts. "I'm not running scared, I just don't see the need to let you paw me whenever you want."

He almost smiled. Actually, he should be highly insulted. Women begged for his touch, in many different ways. But Darci was innocent, he reminded himself. He'd known that the first time they'd kissed. She might not necessarily be a virgin, but she'd never truly explored her sexuality with a man. And no man had ever allowed her the full release she deserved.

"Does my touch repulse you?" Gently, firmly, he pried her hand free and curled her small fingers into his. The brief brush against her silk-covered breast was almost his undoing, but he concentrated on the night noises around them, forcing his body back under control.

"Of course not." She tentatively tugged on her hand, then gave up.

He moved a little closer, just close enough to catch an occasional whiff of her perfume, just close enough to torture himself with the possibilities.

Darci shrugged. "It's just that this . . . this marriage isn't what I was expecting."

"What were you expecting?"

"I don't know." Her lips twisted ruefully. "You didn't give me much time to think about it, did you."

"There wasn't time to give." And if he'd allowed her any time, she would never have gone through with the deed. Especially if she'd had time to find out about his true motives. "It's okay, honey. We'll make it all work."

He watched as she swallowed her doubts, and he resisted the urge to breathe a sigh of relief. He'd always planned ahead at the rodeo, had watched the calves run, plotted the course of his rope, thought every move through. Everything else in his life had been accomplished with the same carefully timed precision.

For once he was running blind, and so far, it was working. He could only hope it would continue to fall into place. Because for once, he didn't have a clue what the next step was. And failure would cost him more than he'd ever had to lose.

The evening activity swirled around them as they walked. Cole let it all slide past him, aware only of the woman—the little girl who had unexpectedly grown up—walking at his side.

Darci suddenly stopped and turned away from him to look into a darkened store window. Cole could see her watching him in the glass, trying to gauge his intentions. "So what are the rules of this relationship?"

He adjusted his hat, playing for time. Now was his chance to make their relationship a real marriage. He could convince her, could kiss her into submission. Because he knew that he could bring her the ultimate satisfaction.

But he hesitated. It didn't feel right. Just physical satisfaction wasn't what he wanted with Darci. He wanted more from their relationship, but his heart shied away from admitting how far he was willing to take this marriage.

Finally, he knew he couldn't delay any longer. "What do you want the rules to be?"

A slight smile touched her lips. "What? No battle lines, no ultimatums, no demands?"

He lifted his hands to rest on her shoulders and pulled her back to lean against his chest. "What I want is what's best for both of us, Darci. And we need to find out what that is."

Closing his eyes briefly, he let her hair stroke his cheek, let himself wallow in her softness. "We need to be able to touch each other, look at each other and talk to each other like we're madly in love. Can you do it?"

She studied him carefully in the glass. "I think so. You're an attractive man. It'll be no hardship to let myself think you're mine."

"You were always reserved as a child, always held a piece of yourself apart from the world. You can't do that with a husband, honey. You have to act like we're intimately acquainted, not only with each other's thoughts and dreams, but with each other's bodies.''

A faint blush tinged her cheeks, but she didn't look away.

''Otherwise, Anita and Uncle John will get their way and we'll lose it all.'' He waited for her response, the ticking seconds making him tense. It was worse than waiting for the starting signal before a big competition.

Slowly, she turned in his arms and lifted her face to his. ''Teach me, Cole. Teach me how to act, how to love.''

He wanted desperately to take her words literally, but knew she didn't mean what she said. He lowered his head and touched his lips to hers for a brief second. The brim of his hat shadowed them, offering a false intimacy, something he was more than willing to take advantage of after tasting her again.

Gently nibbling the softness offered to him, he deepened the kiss and pulled her closer. She melted against him, her sigh a brush of satisfaction against his face. She wanted him as much as he wanted her, she just didn't know it yet. It was up to him to teach her, to lead the way. It might be the purest form of agony, but he would go slowly.

Pulling his mouth from hers, he tucked her head against his chest, willing his heart to slow its frantic pace.

''Was that in the rules or did we just cheat?'' Cole asked.

He chuckled, regretting the words that needed to be said. But it was for his sake as well as hers. Because he suspected it would be too easy to become attached to Darci; he was dangerously close already.

''Okay, here's how the game will be played. We won't consummate the marriage, only act like we have.'' The tone of his voice shifted, deepened into a husky rasp he couldn't control. "We'll act the part of lovebirds in public, but it's hands-off in private. Otherwise, we might be tempted to break the rules."

She squirmed and tried to lift her head, but he held her still with one large hand. If he saw the passion he'd sparked reflected in her eyes, nothing could stop him from dragging her back to the hotel for a proper wedding night.

"Wait, Darci. Listen to me." She quieted, and he stroked her hair, gently pulling the golden strands loose from the tight confines.

"You're still too much of a stranger for me to think of you in that way." The lie twisted through him, searing his insides. "Let's spend some time getting used to each other, and we'll discuss any changes either of us wants to make as they come up."

Her fingers tangled with the pearl button of his shirt, and the sensation shot straight through him. "So we're just good friends, but need to act like lovers?"

To distract himself, he pulled the few remaining pins from her hair. He fluffed the golden strands across her shoulders, savoring the softness.

"Exactly. No demands, no expectations, unless we discuss it first. Okay?" He tilted her chin up and looked at her, delighted at the traces of regret he saw mirrored in her face. Then she smiled and he couldn't resist smiling back.

"So I can touch you whenever and wherever I want in public, but it's hands-off in the confines of our own home, right?" She pushed her hair out of her face, tucking one strand behind her ear.

"It's a little backward, I know, but we've never managed a normal relationship yet, so why should we start now?"

"Why indeed?" She pulled away and took his hand in hers. "Well, Mr. Blackmore, what would you like to see tonight?"

What he really wanted to see couldn't be viewed on a public street, so he directed his attention to the job of convincing the world they were married. Lifting her hand, he kissed the backs of her fingers. "I think a wedding ring is in order, Mrs. Blackmore. Are there any jewelry stores nearby?"

"Oh, no. That's too expensive. I'll just pick something out of my jewelry box and put it on my left hand. No one will know the difference."

"I'll know."

"Cole, neither of us has any money to waste right now. The company needs every penny."

His teeth clenched, and he forced himself not to think of the stack of medical bills still waiting to be paid. "My wife will have a proper ring. End of discussion."

Silence greeted his words, and he waited for the explosion.

"You're not going to get away with that every time," she finally said.

"Get away with what?"

"The 'Me Tarzan, You Jane' act. I will be an equal partner in this arrangement, and I will take an active part in all decisions." She turned and walked backward in front of him, laughter lighting her eyes. "But I'll give in just this once, because I really would like a wedding ring."

The little girl was there again, peeking out, desperately asking for approval, love and acceptance. He only hoped he didn't manage to crush the last of her innocence in his desperate bid to save himself.

He tried twice before he could get out his next sentence in the lighthearted vein he knew was necessary right now. "Lead me to a jewelry store and we'll find a rock the size of Gibraltar for you. Something big enough that we'll need to buy a little horse for you to rest your hand on."

She turned to walk beside him again, both hands wrapped around his work-roughened fingers. "The cleaning service at the office will never put up with that. Can you imagine the damage even a little horse would do to the beige carpet?"

Unable to resist, he bent and pressed a quick kiss on her smiling lips—trying to absorb her laughter and warmth, to draw it deep into the cold places around his heart. A flash of heat darted through him, but as soon as he pulled away from her, the cold returned, settling in deeper than before.

He wanted Darci's sunshine, her love, but he couldn't allow himself to reach out for it. He would only destroy it, the same way he'd destroyed his first wife. And he couldn't bear to see Darci without the joy of life sparkling in her eyes.

Darci stopped suddenly, and Cole looked up to see a discreet jeweler's sign over a lighted canopy. "This place is a little expensive, but it's the best choice downtown. Maybe we should wait until tomorrow and go to the mall."

Cole clenched his teeth to hold back the reply he wanted to make. He was feeling more like a beggar relative with each passing moment. He, Cole Blackmore, the toast of the rodeo circuit, the man with the golden rope and a talent for making money grow, was having trouble accepting his new reality.

And the reality was he couldn't afford even the simplest diamond for his wife.

"This is perfect." He dragged her inside before she could protest.

An older, well-dressed man came forward to help them. After they told him what they were looking for, the clerk directed them to a glass case. As Cole stood looking down into the trays of gaudy rings, his common sense finally prevailed. He'd have to let his pride go, would have to find another way. The mere fact that none of these rings sported price tags told him he couldn't afford even the simplest setting.

Somehow, Darci seemed to sense the despair curling through him. She gazed at the display case for a long minute, then grinned brightly at the clerk. "These just aren't my style. Thank you." Before the clerk could protest, she dragged Cole from the store.

He tried to pull her to a stop, but she charged forward like a horse with the scent of home in its nose. "Darci, wait." She pulled her hand from his and kept walking, her steps clipping angrily on the sidewalk. "Honey, what's the matter?"

Finally, he caught her shoulder and spun her around to face him. A single tear glistened on the edge of her eyelashes causing a knife of pain in his heart that almost brought him to his knees. Catching the crystal drop on his finger, he waited.

"You can't afford a ring any more than I can. It was all a scam, wasn't it? The offer to buy me out, to make me a rich woman, it was a lie."

He opened his mouth to protest, then closed it when she rushed on.

"If we have nothing else between us, Cole, we have to be honest with each other. Do you have any money?"

The lie crowded his vocal cords, demanding to be said. He could lead her on, make her believe he was still a wealthy man, still capable of saving their company. His silver tongue had told bigger lies, woven more complicated stories. But this was Darci, the only person who had ever believed in him no matter what he did.

"Honey, my wallet's flatter than a pancake. I've got enough to support...myself, but there's not enough for even the smallest frills."

"What happened to it all—the success, the endorsements, the big purses?"

He tipped his head back to stare at the sky, looking for the right words. "It's a long story, and I'm not sure I'm ready to share it just yet. Is that okay?"

She searched his face, probed his eyes, looking for the truth. Finally, she nodded, once. "It'll do for now. But no more stories. If you don't want to tell me, just say so. Don't make something up. Is that clear?"

He almost smiled, his relief was so great. She wasn't ready to judge him and she wasn't demanding answers he wasn't ready to give. Maybe she would understand when she finally met Mandy. "Yes, it's very clear." He wove her fingers through his, enjoying the feel of her delicate bone structure. "But that still leaves us with the matter of a ring."

"I know just the place." She started forward, towing him behind. He was beginning to feel like a horse on a lead, but what really bothered him was that he was actually starting to like it.

The neighborhood quickly deteriorated, and Cole wondered about the wisdom of giving Darci her head. Her fingers tightened around his, letting him know she was uncomfortable with their surroundings, too. Finally, she stopped in front of a battered storefront, then went inside.

A burly old man was standing behind the counter of the pawn shop. "Can I help you?"

"We need to look at wedding rings, please." Darci's voice echoed around the old room, the cavernous depths absorbing the slight quiver Cole felt transmitted through her fingers.

The old man grinned. "Newlyweds, right? Just eloped with no thought of what needed to be done, huh?"

Darci didn't seem able to answer, so Cole stepped in. He draped his arm across her shoulders, tugging her closer to his side. "We couldn't wait another day, but I want her to have a nice ring to show all her friends tomorrow. Have anything special?"

The man chuckled as he leaned under the counter. "Me and the missus eloped, too. Best thing we ever did. Been married almost forty years now and never regretted a day of it."

Forty years. An eternity. Cole tried to tune out the old man's reminiscences. Dreams were all he had, dreams of sharing and loving the right person, dreams that would never come true. He couldn't allow them to come true or the wrong people would get hurt.

Quickly he scanned the rings displayed in front of them. One caught his eye, and he plucked it from the black velvet. The setting was old, ornate, with a small diamond nestled in the fine scrolling. It reminded Cole of lasting love, of deep abiding faith in one's mate. The fact that the ring was in a pawn shop mocked him, but he shoved the idea aside.

"We'll take this one if that's okay with you, honey."

Darci looked up at him with shining eyes. "It's beautiful...perfect."

The clerk took Cole's check, then beamed at them. "Take her outside and put it on her finger. Then you can kiss her properly to seal the deal." He winked at them. "Enjoy your wedding night, folks." Discreetly, he turned away to dust another counter.

Cole led Darci outside, then stopped and took her left hand into his. Slowly, he slipped the ring on and wasn't overly surprised when it fit perfectly. He had known the ring belonged on Darci's hand the moment he'd seen it.

With the proof of his vows safely on her finger, he pulled her into his arms for another kiss. He knew better, knew he was tempting fate, playing with a fire that could easily burn out of his control, but he needed to drink from her vitality just once more.

Desire went through him like a flash fire, burning away his common sense. He deepened the kiss, needing to feel her pressed against him, wanting to torment himself with a desire that would go unfulfilled. Their tongues met, melded, and he had a sudden sense of coming home.

When he finally pulled away, she sighed and nestled her head against his chest. "Cole?"

"Yes?" His fingers tangled in her hair, clutching at something he knew he couldn't have, while he struggled to slow his breathing.

"How long do we stay married? How long does it last?" Her voice was a bare thread of sound.

He closed his eyes as the despair washed over him again. He had no choice; all roads had been blocked except this one. The only option was to take it and see where it led while trying not to hurt Darci. "As long as we need to, honey. Trust me, we'll work it out."

The words seemed to echo around him. He'd said them over and over, to her and to himself. But deep down he wasn't certain he could be trusted. He no longer understood his own motives.

Her fingers curled against his neck, and she clung to him, transmitting her doubts as surely as if she'd said them aloud. A flood of possessiveness washed through him.

She was his. His woman. His wife.

And suddenly, Cole knew he was in very big trouble. He was beginning to want more than a temporary wife, beginning to want Darci by his side for a lifetime.

Chapter Four

The night air washed across Darci's face as they strolled the emptying streets back to Cole's hotel. Neither spoke, and Darci hadn't a clue how to break the growing silence. There were things that needed to be said between them, but too much stood in the way of the saying.

She twisted at her wedding ring aimlessly, trying to adjust to the unfamiliar weight on her finger, to what it symbolized. Somehow, it had all become very real in these past few minutes. She was married to the man of her dreams, but she'd never be allowed to love him the way she'd always known she could.

Because to love Cole would surely lead to a heartbreak she wouldn't survive.

Cole stepped into the lobby and tugged her toward the elevator. Dragging him to a stop, she waited until he turned to look at her with a question shading his gray eyes.

"I think it's time I say good-night."

He frowned, then drew her closer, tucking her into his arms. "I thought we should make some plans, discuss the next step."

Darci shook her head, knowing she didn't dare be alone with him yet. She needed him too badly, and her exhaustion made it difficult for her to form the words that she had to say. "Come to my office in the morning, we'll talk then."

"But what about—"

She placed her cold fingers against his lips, absorbing his warmth. "I can't deal with any more, Cole. Too much has happened too quickly, and I need some time to assimilate all of it." His protest still lingered in his eyes. "Please?"

His lips pursed, and he pressed a gentle kiss against her fingertips, sending a shaft of longing straight to her soul. She clenched her teeth, resisting the urge to follow through with what she really wanted from Cole.

"You're right. We both need time. Unfortunately, that isn't something we have a lot of. By tomorrow night, we need to be living together, acting like a loving husband and wife, and making some serious plans."

"I know. And we will. Just give me tonight." Her words became a double-edged sword that she suspected he was sharing with her. She wanted to give him the night, to share the darkness with him and learn the secrets of his body. But thoughts and feelings of that nature would only lead to serious trouble.

His arms remained around her, and she waited, not certain he would release her, tantalized by the thought that he wouldn't.

"Darci, what do you want from this relationship?"

His question made her thoughts spin. *I want love— lifetime, lasting love. I want to be needed, to have a safe haven.* The words echoed through her heart, accenting the longing she'd struggled with for so many years. But she held the thought deep inside, knowing she couldn't share the words. Not now. Not ever.

She forced a smile to her lips. "I want to save Blackmore's, of course. That's all that matters to me." For the first time, the words rang hollow. "And you?"

Through the shadow of his hat brim, she saw something flicker in his eyes, but it was so quick, she didn't have a chance to define it. "The same thing, honey. The very same thing."

His arms loosened and he stepped back. Darci turned and walked slowly to the revolving door, regret sounding in every step. Why shouldn't she stay with him? They were married, it was morally and legally acceptable. And her body burned for his touch.

But the price was too high; she couldn't afford to take the chance. Cole was just another man who wanted to use her for his own gain, the same way Jeffrey had. At least Cole had been honest about his plans. Jeffrey had deceived her from the first. And she'd never craved Jeffrey's touch like she did Cole's.

Somehow, she made it home, her thoughts a whirling jumble of confusion. When she unlocked the door to her condo, she tried to imagine Cole there, to feel his presence. But he didn't fit. He was a man who needed the open range, the freedom of a cowboy's life. He'd stagnate in the city. Another reason not to get too attached to the man. Their lives were headed in very different directions.

Scruffy was there to greet her as usual, but tonight, it only intensified Darci's loneliness. Taking the little dog to bed with her, she pulled him close, knowing he was a very poor substitute for what she wanted.

The long night passed in a blur of longing for what she couldn't have. Cole's touch haunted her, and she remembered the texture of his skin, the scent that was uniquely his.

The next morning, Darci repeated the ritual of trying to hide the ravages of little sleep, but with no more success than before. The staff would begin to think she led a wild nightlife if this continued much longer.

She fiddled with the papers on her desk until almost ten o'clock, the disappointment, the nagging doubts, growing when Cole didn't seek her out. Maybe he'd found a more interesting distraction. Maybe he hadn't meant anything he'd said about working by her side to save their shared heritage.

Maybe this was proof of what she'd heard about Cole so many years ago. Cole's father had always said Cole was unreliable, unable to stay focused on what needed to be done. But that didn't fit with the image Darci had of a champion rodeo cowboy. It took guts, determination and a total single-mindedness to get as far in the rodeo world as Cole had.

Finally, after an eternity of doubts, Alex buzzed her office and informed her Cole was on the phone. Warmth flowed through her just at the thought of talking with her new husband. Eagerly, Darci lifted the receiver, forcing aside the unnamed fears that had built up over the past hour.

He didn't offer any excuse or greeting. "Darci, I won't be able to come to the office today. Something's come up." His voice held an unnatural strain.

There was a pause, a perfect opportunity for her to express her anger, her frustration, to demand answers. Instead, she responded to his tense tone, knowing this wasn't the time to challenge him. She needed to believe Cole wouldn't do anything without good reason, that he cared enough not to hurt her. She had to believe that or she wouldn't be able to continue with their charade. So she simply gripped the receiver tighter and waited for him to continue.

His sigh transmitted across the line. "Give me your address and I'll meet you at your place as soon as I can."

Refusal hovered on her lips, but her desperate need to believe in someone overrode the words. Like it or not, she needed Cole. And she'd have to put up with whatever he dished out to accomplish her goals. She simply had to remember what those goals were, had to focus on what she'd wanted before Cole stampeded back into her life.

"I may have to work late tonight."

"No problem. How about if I meet you at the office later, when I can get away?"

Without warning, her eyes filled with tears. She nodded, swallowing to clear her voice. "Bring something to eat. I'm sure we'll both be hungry." She set the phone down just before the tears escaped. Silently, she wept for her childhood dreams, dreams that kept slipping farther out of her reach with each passing day. She just wanted to be loved, to be needed by someone.

When a knock sounded at her door, Darci grabbed a tissue and, with a final sniff, erased all traces of her tears. "Come in."

Alex poked his head into the room. "Is Mr. Blackmore going to be in today?"

She resented having to make excuses for Cole, no matter what his reason for not being here. "No, Alex. He's been delayed. Is his office ready?"

Alex nodded. "And I've selected Mrs. Jackson as his secretary."

Darci stifled a moan. She would have preferred someone older, someone more experienced. Experience to the devil, she would have preferred anyone but the pretty widow who had substituted for Alex when he went on vacation. But the woman was very competent, and Darci couldn't fault Alex's choice based on how the woman looked.

Darci frowned over the jealousy churning through her. Cole hadn't even met the woman, had done nothing to make her distrust him. But suddenly, Darci was feeling very possessive of her temporary husband. This unexpected whirl of emotions was destroying her sanity.

She forced her usual businesslike tone of voice. "Just have her get his office organized for today and I'm certain he'll be in tomorrow."

Alex nodded again and began to close the door. Leaning back into the room, he said, "Maybe a glass of wine tonight would help you get some sleep."

Darci tried to smile her thanks for the suggestion. Somehow, she doubted an entire bottle of wine would help. With Cole in the next room, she didn't think sleep would come easily. Which meant she could look forward to another day of mind-numbing exhaustion. If she didn't get her act together soon, the company would slip from her fingers while she was taking an unscheduled nap.

Forcing her mind to the work needing to be done, she picked up her pen and flipped open a file. But all she could think of was Cole—his touch, his kiss, the desperate need she saw lingering deep in his eyes, the need that matched her own.

She sighed just as the intercom buzzed. With a punch of her finger, she took out a small portion of her frustration on the helpless button. "Yes, Alex?"

"Jeffrey is on the line."

Darci squeezed the bridge of her nose, trying to stave off the headache building there. She'd told Jeffrey never to call again, but the man was being very persistent. Of course, he had a lot to lose by letting her slip away from him. He'd all but admitted to it the night she'd given back the ring. "Tell him I'm in a meeting, please."

"This is the fourth time he's called in two days."

"I know, Alex. I'll deal with him soon. Just indulge me one more time."

"Yes, ma'am."

Darci almost smiled when she heard the line disconnect. Alex's voice should have reflected irritation at having to do her dirty work for her. But she detected a certain relish in his tone, almost as if he was looking forward to thwarting Jeffrey one more time.

Had she been the only one who had fallen for the man's false charm? Darci's mother had approved of the marriage, and Darci suspected it had little to do with love and happily-ever-after.

The conspiracy she'd sensed hovering in the background of her life months ago drew closer, filling Darci with a sense of urgency. She needed more time, she needed help.

Heaven help her, she needed Cole.

The small hand twitched against his fingers, and Cole jerked awake. He reached out to smooth the tangled curls from Mandy's face, watching her intently. Relief flooded him as her eyelids flickered open and she peeked at him with a wobbly smile.

After seven long months of operations, of hoping and praying, he'd finally thought they were over the danger. He'd thought he could relax and simply help Mandy get her strength back. But he'd been wrong. "Hi, Snuggle-bug. How are you feeling?"

"Funny. I don't like it."

He'd give anything to ease her pain. But that simply wasn't in his power. He was again faced with the fact that he was a mere mortal and he was stuck with having to deal with whatever obstacles the gods chose to throw into his life. It was an all-too-familiar emotion that had visited him frequently since his wife died in the same accident that had almost taken Mandy from him.

"I'm sorry." His words seemed so inadequate. "Can I get you anything?"

"I just wanna sleep," Mandy mumbled.

"And that's just what you should do." He squeezed her hand. "I'll be right here if you need me." His heart wrenched as her eyes drifted closed.

The message had been waiting for him last night when he got back to the hotel room. Mandy had been staying with friends in the foothills west of Denver while Cole tried to straighten out their lives. He had talked to her every day on the phone, but he had missed her desperately.

Then last night, Mandy had experienced an allergic reaction to a new pain medication and been rushed to the hospital. Cole had been forced to wait helplessly during the agonizing hours until she'd been stabilized. When she'd actually stopped breathing for a few seconds, Cole had experienced more agony than he thought was possible for a man to bear.

Cole shifted in the chair, trying to ease the pain settling into his injured hip. He'd almost lost her. Again. He didn't know how much more of this he could take.

The accident had almost taken her away once, but she'd pulled through. The healing was a long, slow process, but the doctors continually assured him she would be normal again, that she would run and laugh and play just like other kids. But it would take time. And during that time, they had to deal with the pain Mandy's recovering body was going through.

The endless night had been filled with a terror that ran deep while his daughter struggled against her own body's reaction to the medicine. Mandy was the only thing that made him feel alive anymore, the only reason he got out of bed each morning.

Except for Darci. He suspected she could make him care, something he couldn't allow himself to do.

He bowed his head over their clasped hands. He'd given up on praying when Sharon died. But he'd do anything for Mandy, had already done the unacceptable by marrying Darci for his own selfish needs. Maybe it was time to try asking for help from a higher source. Maybe it was time to believe that there was someone or something out there that could help him.

Because he needed to believe that there was a chance for them, for all three of them. He needed to believe he was doing the right thing, that there was some method to the madness his life had deteriorated to.

He glanced out the window at the afternoon sun, scrubbing a hand over his face. The last weeks had allowed him little sleep. Maybe his exhaustion was affecting his judgment. Maybe he'd just dug himself a hole deeper than anything he could ever hope to crawl out of.

* * *

The sun was already slipping behind the Rocky Mountains when he finally left the hospital. Mandy was out of danger, and the doctor had all but thrown Cole out, demanding he get some rest, too.

The large office building that housed Blackmore's Gourmet Chocolates was silent except for Cole's footsteps echoing through the hall. Darci's image teased his exhausted thoughts, tempting him, drawing him to her. A cold fear etched its way through the darkness inside him as he realized that he was looking forward to seeing her.

Easing the door of Darci's office open, he watched her work, remembering a night just a few days ago when he'd stood in the same place. But so much had changed since then. That first night, he'd been looking for a way to survive, a way to help Mandy. And Darci had simply been a means to an end. Until he'd seen her smile, until she'd managed to touch his frozen heart.

She was now his wife. He couldn't seem to stop himself from caring about her, about what happened to her when he left. And he couldn't stop wanting her in ways a husband had every right to want his wife.

He clamped his eyes shut on the feelings washing through him. He couldn't stop to analyze them now, didn't dare even acknowledge the more tender thoughts. Instead, he tried to cover his emotions with anger.

"You should keep the outer door locked. Anyone could walk in here, and you wouldn't even notice until it was too late."

Darci jumped, scattering papers to the floor, her eyes wide when she looked up at him. He allowed himself the small satisfaction of knowing he'd scared her enough that she might be more careful next time.

"Cole, don't sneak up on me like that."

"Better me than someone else." He threw his hat onto the leather couch and glared at her. A frown traced a small crease between her eyebrows as she studied him. When the little girl peeked out for reassurance, his anger evaporated as quickly as it had come. He held up a white paper bag, forcing his lips into a smile. "Chinese okay?"

She joined him on the couch, and he suffered the brush of her hands, the scent of her delicate perfume and the softness of her voice while they ate. He carefully kept the conversation on business, admiring her ideas as she tried to explain what she wanted to accomplish in the next few months.

"So the magical world of candy-making hasn't changed all that much over the years, has it?"

Darci shook her head. "Blackmore's hasn't changed a bit. And we need to. There's new equipment out, more aggressive marketing techniques, even new products. We're still doing the same things we were doing twenty years ago, but it's not working anymore and no one on the board will recognize that."

"It's not going to be easy to convince the board that this is the best thing, you know." Frustration shadowed her eyes at his words.

"I know. They're afraid to try anything new. But if we keep going the way we have for the last few years, there won't be a company to worry about. We can't keep up with the competition anymore. It's time for change."

He put his hand over hers, offering his support, trying to ignore the energy pulsing between them. "If we could get Anita and Uncle John on our side there would be no problem, the board would have to go with it. They seem set against anything you want to do. Why is that?"

Darci's laugh was touched with a trace of bitterness. "It was your father's wish that I run the company, and the board has so far honored that request, although they seem reluctant at times. I want to change the way things have always been done, and that scares them.

"Uncle John has wanted control since before Daddy died, and he resents my being in his way."

Cole shook his head, thinking back to the arguments between John and Cole's father over John's lack of interest in their business. "He never cared about the company before, never wanted anything to do with it. I can't imagine him sitting in the president's seat."

"Oh, he doesn't want to run it. At least not actively. He's already announced that he wants to help select the new president, someone who will do things the right way." Darci's mouth turned into a grim smile. "In other words, he wants someone who will do things his way, instead of thinking for themselves."

Cole pulled his hand away from hers on the pretext of continuing with his meal. But he was forced to admit to himself that he couldn't take the feel of her skin any longer without turning his touch into a caress.

"Uncle John's managed to convince Mother that I'll never settle down to marry and raise a family as long as I have all this glamour and excitement to keep me distracted from finding the right man."

Cole grinned in spite of the desire churning through him. "But you are married now. And we'll work on the settling down part."

Darci flashed him a reluctant smile. "But you're not the perfect man Mother chose for me. Her candidate has lost out. She can't stand to be wrong, if you'll remember."

His jaw clenched at the memories from the short amount of time he'd spent in the presence of Anita Blackmore. Darci was sugar-coating the truth. Anita Blackmore had never entertained the thought that she could possibly be wrong. And the rest of the world was expected to pander to her expectations.

When Darci stood, Cole allowed himself a moment to admire the gentle sway of her hips as she walked back to the desk. The crisp little business suit she wore hinted at undiscovered passions. He wanted to be the one to discover her secrets, to teach her just what love was all about. He let his breath out in a slow, controlled sigh, forcing the tantalizing thought away. He had to concentrate on business.

She sat at the desk and pulled the last file folder closer. "Thanks for dinner, Cole. Let me finish reading this last report and then we'll head for home."

Home. The word had an odd ring to it and brought a feeling of wistfulness to Cole. He wasn't used to these emotions. For too many years, he'd just been trying to succeed in a tough world and hadn't had time to feel. Then he'd held his newborn daughter in his arms, and the world championship he'd just won paled in comparison. But he'd been certain he had the world by the tail.

As fate often decreed, his marriage and his career had fallen apart, and he'd struggled to survive the challenges that were thrown his way. He'd closed off his heart and his feelings. Now the unexpected emotions battered him, threatening to tear him apart.

He sat on the leather couch and watched Darci. Her hair was loose around her shoulders, and the soft lighting glinted off the golden highlights. Desire curled through him as he began to weave a fantasy life that could never exist for either of them. To have a real marriage, a normal life, happy children and a home. It was something that had always been held just out of his reach until he'd given up on it.

But Darci brought the old wants back to torment him.

The office door popped open without warning and a well-dressed man walked in as if he belonged there. Cole tensed, looking back and forth between Darci and the newcomer. Darci hadn't been very talkative about her past relationships, but Cole suspected he was about to learn more than if she'd told him her version of the facts.

"Jeffrey, what are you doing here?"

"You've been avoiding me. We need to talk." Jeffrey braced his arms on the desk and leaned toward Darci.

"We've already said everything that can be said months ago. Now, please leave, Jeffrey, I have work to do." Darci's voice carried a coldness that Cole hadn't thought she was capable of.

"You've said what you wanted to say. I was never allowed to present my side."

"You mean you weren't allowed to distort the facts, to try to convince me I didn't see what I did?" She spread her hands on the desk. "How do you explain away that woman, what magic words do you use to make her disappear?"

Cole stood, fighting his protective urges, when Jeffrey grabbed Darci by the shoulders, forcing her up to his level. "You can't throw our love away that easily."

"What we had obviously wasn't love. You never loved me, or even cared enough to consider my feelings. Good night, Jeffrey." Darci shook herself free of his grip, but he reached for her again.

Closing the distance between them quickly, Cole tapped the man on the shoulder and waited for him to turn. "I believe the lady has made herself clear. Get out."

"Who the hell are you?" The words were a direct challenge.

Cole eyed the man, almost relishing the thought of planting a fist in Jeffrey's stomach. "I'm her husband." He was surprised at the satisfaction the words brought him. "Who are you?"

The shock filtered through Jeffrey's eyes as he stared at Cole. With a trace of panic in his actions, Jeffrey spun around to glare at Darci. "I'm her fiancé. What's going on here?"

Darci had a sudden urge to crawl under the desk and pretend they couldn't see her. But that was a game that hadn't worked even when she was young enough to believe it would.

The hurt she'd felt at Jeffrey's betrayal five months ago gave her the strength to say what needed to be said. "Cole and I were married yesterday." At Jeffrey's shocked gasp, she added lamely, "It was a rather sudden thing."

"Darci, you can't do this. You made a promise to me. You owe me."

She stared at him for several seconds, trying to sort through his flawed logic. "You broke your end of the bargain, Jeffrey. I owe you nothing."

Something flickered in Jeffrey's eyes as he glared at the newlyweds. "Something isn't right. It's all a scam. And that means that when it all comes out, your motives will be no better than mine."

She winced at his words, afraid that he might be right, hating the thought that she might have stooped to his level to get what she wanted.

"I'll be back, Darci. Count on it. I still intend to have you as my wife and this company as my livelihood." Jeffrey spun and strode from the room. Sparing one final glare for Cole, Jeffrey slammed the door behind him.

Darci slowly sank into the chair.

"Life a little complicated right now?"

The amusement in Cole's voice almost released the hysteria building inside her. Darci dropped her head in her hands and drew in a deep, calming breath.

"For a girl who rarely even dated, how did I end up with two men suddenly wanting to be married to me?"

Cole moved behind her and gently massaged the tension from her shoulders. But instead of relaxing her, his touch set fire to her skin, making her want to lean back into his hands. Possibilities for the night ahead teased her, but she tried to push them aside, knowing there was important work to be done.

"It must be that fantastic smile."

She couldn't stop the bitterness. "It must be Blackmore's Gourmet Chocolates. The illusion of power does amazing things to people."

Cole's hands dropped away, and Darci felt a flash of guilt. Slowly, she turned in her chair until she was facing him. The expression on his face made her uneasy. "I didn't mean—"

"Yes, you did. And it's the truth. I married you for the company. But I do care for you." His hand curved around her cheek as his lips formed a lopsided grin. "I don't love you, but we both knew that going into this mess."

She waited, for something, anything, her heart thudding heavily at his touch.

"Can he hurt us?"

Darci blinked, trying to sort through the physical sensations bombarding her and focus on the meaning of his words. "No, I don't think he can. He was on Mother's side when it came to running the business, but he doesn't have the power to do anything now."

Cole nodded in satisfaction as his fingers traced a path over her skin. "Tell me about what happened with Jeffrey."

She started to feel claustrophobic. Gulping at the air that seemed to be disappearing at an alarming rate, she gasped, "I'd rather not."

"Darci, if I'm going to help you slay these dragons, I need to know how dangerous they are. What happened?"

Almost desperate to be free of the sensations flaring through her, she jumped up and turned to face the window, her arms hugged across her stomach. "He only slept with another woman. And I made the mistake of walking in on them." Her laugh echoed with the agony of the betrayal.

"I was going to surprise him with a late dinner, but I was the one who got the surprise. When I threw his ring at him and left, he had the audacity to follow me home, thinking he could explain it away. But a naked woman in his apartment was a little difficult to justify, even to someone as naive and trusting as I am."

Darci sucked in a ragged breath, trying to hold off the pain. "We ended up in a shouting match, and he told me he was only marrying me for the company, anyway, so it didn't make any difference." She swallowed, trying to remove the emotions quivering in her voice. "But it did make a difference. I thought I loved him, and it hurt to find out it was all a sham."

Cole's hands settled on her shoulders, and very gently he turned her around. His lips touched her hair, drifting down to her forehead before touching her lips. Nibbling and coaxing, he encouraged her to open her mouth to him.

Ignoring the warnings flashing through her thoughts, she gave herself over to his touch. When his tongue delved inside to meet hers, all thoughts of Jeffrey fled from her mind. Wrapping her arms around his neck, she pulled Cole closer, desperate for his warmth, his strength. She needed to feel wanted, and Cole was doing a very good job of accomplishing that right now.

His long fingers traced a path from her shoulders down to the small of her back, then up again. Mindlessly, she let him lead her into deeper kisses, caught up in a heat that threatened to consume her common sense.

Nothing mattered right now, not her mother, not the company. Nothing but Cole's touch, his kiss, his heat.

Suddenly, Cole pulled away. Darci opened her eyes enough to see him through her lashes. Passion ravaged his face and burned his eyes, setting new fires to smolder deep inside her.

"This isn't right." His voice was a husky remnant of his usual tone.

"You're my husband. What could be so wrong about it?" She wanted him like she'd wanted no man in the past, not even Jeffrey. When she felt Cole putting the distance of his withdrawal between them, she struggled not to pull his mouth back down to hers and kiss away any protests he might make.

"Temporary husband. And if we follow through on this, it will only complicate the ending of our little fairy tale."

His logic was worse than a splash of cold water. For just one moment, she'd managed to forget about him leaving. Quickly, she withdrew her arms and tugged at her suit jacket to keep her hands occupied. "You're right. I'm sorry."

He halted her retreat by grabbing her shoulders again, forcing her to look up at him. "I'm not. I want you, don't doubt that for a minute."

He jerked away and stalked over to the couch where he grabbed his hat and shoved it on his head. "I'll wait for you in the hallway. I just need to pick up my suitcase at the hotel and I'll be ready to move in."

He stopped just before the door closed and pushed it back open. The hat shaded his eyes, but his voice was deeper than normal, reflecting an inner struggle that matched Darci's. "Honey, I don't ever want to hurt you."

The door clicked shut behind him, and Darci stood frozen for a short eternity.

You already have, she thought as a single tear traced down her cheek.

What had she done? She'd offered herself to him, all but begged him to make love to her. But worst of all, she'd let him walk away. The kiss would always be there, taunting them with its intensity. She only hoped they could still manage to work together.

Mechanically, she pulled the files on her desk into the semblance of a pile, switched off the desk lamp and swung her purse over her shoulder. With only the moonlight showing her the way, she pulled her door shut behind her and started across the darkened outer office. A loud crash halted her in her tracks, sending a flash of panic through her.

Chapter Five

Concerned only for Cole, she rushed into the hallway, skidding to a horrified stop at the scene waiting for her. Cole stood over Jeffrey, who was lying on the highly polished floor, massaging his jaw. A small vase lay shattered at his side.

"If you think you're man enough, let's try that again." There was a quiet threat in Cole's voice that sent fear skittering over her skin.

"You're nothing but a stupid cowboy. Why don't you go back to the open range where you belong?" Jeffrey dared to rise up on one elbow.

"Don't push your luck, city boy. Darci is now my wife, and I'd suggest you leave her alone." Cole's hands tightened into fists.

Darci quickly stepped beside him and wrapped his hand in hers, trying to keep him from doing any further damage.

When Jeffrey saw her, he eased himself off the floor, dusting his suit off. "I can't imagine what you see in this hick, Darci. When you decide you want a bit more polish in your life, give me a call. There's still time for me to fix everything for you." He turned away, then called over his shoulder, "But don't wait too long, or it might be too late."

Jeffrey stabbed at the elevator button, and Darci couldn't stop her sigh of relief when the doors popped open right away. When Jeffrey had disappeared from their view, she turned to Cole. "What happened?"

Cole's hands flexed, clenched, then relaxed. All signs of violence were gone when he turned to face her. Except for the banked anger lurking in his eyes.

"Don't ask," he ordered.

She opened her mouth to do just that, then thought better of it. There would be time later for questions. For now, she just wanted to get away—from the office problems, from Jeffrey... from the memory of Cole's kiss. Silently, she led the way to the car.

The streetlights flashed on his clenched jaw as she drove to the hotel. The route was familiar; one of her favorite restaurants was in this area, but Darci went slowly, taking each turn with care. She wasn't ready to have him move in yet, wasn't prepared for the intimacy of living in the same house as Cole Blackmore.

She needed more time, time to shore up her defenses, time to build a wall around her heart. Cole's kiss had proven to her just how vulnerable she was to him, how dangerous he was to her.

"Do you really love him?"

She jumped at his words, so absorbed in her own thoughts she'd forgotten he was in the car with her for a moment. "Jeffrey? I thought I did. But that was months ago—before I found out what he was really like." The admission was difficult to make, but she knew it was true. "Maybe I just wanted to be in love so badly that I forced it to happen."

"Does that mean you're one of those fickle women, one who changes her mind with every shift of the wind?"

She started to bristle at his words, then recognized the gentle teasing in his tone. Slowly, she forced her hands to relax on the steering wheel. "Not fickle, just a whole lot smarter now than I was."

She let the silence stretch between them. "Why did you hit him?"

"Do you care?"

Cole massaged his knuckles, and she couldn't decide if he was in pain or if he was looking forward to another chance at Jeffrey.

"About him? No. But I need to know what you're thinking, how you feel about him, about my past relationship."

"He was waiting in the hallway, apparently hoping to have one more chance to talk to you." His laugh was rough, sarcastic. "When I came out, he demanded to talk to you. Alone. He didn't want me to have the chance to influence you in any way. When I told him you didn't want to talk with him, he made some . . . disparaging remarks about you that I took exception to."

Cole shrugged, as if his actions were the most natural thing in the world for him. "So I hit him."

Darci bit back a laugh as warmth swelled inside her. He'd been protecting her, defending her honor. It had been a long time since anyone had cared enough to do that. Not since Daddy . . . She shook off the bittersweet memories of the man who had seen her through her teenaged years. He'd loved her, taken care of her like she was his own daughter.

Pulling to a stop in front of the hotel, she threw a questioning look at Cole. Did he really care? Was there a chance for them to make this work? Was it too much for her to dare a dream of more than the agreed-upon year with Cole?

She shook away the gossamer fantasy before it could even develop. Her sigh filled the car, escaping into the cool evening air as Cole opened the door.

"I'll be right back."

The seconds ticked by, but Darci forced her mind to remain still. It would accomplish nothing to worry the possibilities one more time. Without warning, the back door flew open and a single suitcase dropped inside before Cole joined her again.

"You travel light."

He smiled and agreed, not willing to admit that almost everything he owned was in that suitcase. Other than the truck, a few toys and some sparse furniture stored at a friend's house, he'd sold it all in a desperate attempt to pay some of Mandy's mounting medical bills. An attempt that was doomed to failure because he hadn't even made a dent in what he owed. And now he was doing his best to drag Darci down with him.

Darci drove to her condo and pulled to a stop in front. Cole looked around the complex with interest, anxious to get a glimpse into the woman Darci had become. He was surprised at the simplicity of the building, expecting the elegance she'd grown up with to be reflected in her life now.

But the surprise was a pleasant reminder that Darci was her own person, that she had always had her own way of doing things that rarely matched what the world expected of her. Her marrying him on such short notice was a prime example.

The condo's adobe-style buildings glowed in the night light, blending perfectly with the distant Rocky Mountains as their backdrop. Water ran peacefully in the shadows, and the night was alive with subtle sounds. Cole had the strange sensation he'd found a haven to rest, to heal, to learn to live again.

He grabbed his suitcase to follow Darci, tripping on an unobserved curb when he turned. A low curse slipped from his mouth, and he struggled to hide the pain shooting through his still-healing hip. Sweat broke out on his skin with the effort, but the pain faded into a dull ache at Darci's touch.

"Are you all right?"

The concern in her voice soothed him, offered him fresh hope. "I guess I'm getting a little tired. I wasn't watching where I was going and wrenched my leg."

She didn't gush, didn't fuss, simply took his hand and led the way to her section of the building. He followed almost eagerly, wanting to see more, to learn all he could about this woman.

His new wife was like a many-faceted crystal. Each time he looked at her, he found a new sparkle, a new perspective, a fresh delight. And he wanted to keep looking until he knew everything there was to know about her. Then he'd have the memories to savor later when he was alone, when he was wondering how to proceed with a life that seemed to have little direction beyond the deadline of their short-term marriage and his concern over Mandy.

A small fountain splashed in the entryway of her condo, explaining the water sounds he found so soothing. She released his hand to fit the key in the lock and he fought against the sensation of missing her warmth.

"It's so quiet here." He didn't want to go inside yet, didn't want to begin the awkwardness he knew was inevitable while they learned how to live together. Even roommates took time to adjust to each other, and the two of them had so many more issues to deal with. The attraction humming between them became harder to ignore with each passing second.

She hesitated, then took a step back to join him. "It's very isolated. One of the reasons I bought a place here was the assurance of open space all around us. Wildlife from the foothills wanders through here, and there's space to walk, to dream."

The restlessness he'd been fighting since his injury settled into a desperate longing. He was used to traveling, to being on the road constantly during the season. Sharon and Mandy had always shared that life with him, but they'd never managed to become a part of it. But now he wanted to stay in one place for a while.

And he wanted to share that place with Darci.

She finally opened the door and motioned him inside. As she flipped on lights, he looked around, trying to get a measure of her. The inside reflected the Southwestern flavor of the building, making him feel welcome and comfortable.

Suddenly, a white ball of fluff darted from the corner, barking furiously at Cole. He grinned at the ferocious growls and leaned down to make friends. The dog froze, backed up, then finally crept forward to sniff Cole's fingertips cautiously. After a long hesitation, the animal allowed Cole to scratch its head.

"That's Scruffy, my not-so-vicious watchdog." Darci frowned at Cole. "She normally doesn't let anyone but me touch her. You must be a sorcerer or something."

Cole scooped the dog into his arms and grinned. "Animals like me. Maybe because I spend more time with them than I do with humans."

Scruffy snuggled closer, and Cole looked around the room as he rubbed the scraggly fur on the dog's back. The small jungle of plants arranged around the edges of the open room fascinated him. It was a sure sign of Darci's nurturing side, a side that was not being put to good use.

Darci needed a family, someone to care for besides a business that might well reject her. She'd be good for Mandy, would understand the girl's needs better than Cole could ever hope to. But if Darci and Mandy became attached to each other, it would be impossible to walk away at the end of the year. And he'd promised Darci he would walk away, had promised to release her from her vows so she could pursue the life she deserved, could find a man to start a family with. But the thought of her in another man's arms tore at his insides, leaving him shaking with an undirected anger.

"I . . . uh, don't have two beds."

He turned at her words, desperate to reassure her, but not knowing how. *Keep it casual,* he ordered himself. "The couch will do for now. I can sleep just about anywhere."

He would delight in sleeping in her bed, would be content just to hold her in his arms all night, to savor her warmth and her sunshine. But he didn't dare, knew better than to tempt himself or fate with those possibilities.

The kiss he'd shared with Darci earlier had proved one thing. Darci was a beautiful, desirable woman who held deeply buried passions. Passions that he wanted to light a match to while he fanned the flames of her desires to a flash point of ecstasy.

Cole shifted uncomfortably as his jeans grew tighter. He'd have to cease any thoughts in that direction or he'd never make it through the night, much less the next year. *Think of Mandy.* The words rang through his head, but did little to cool his ardor.

"Okay, if you're certain. Maybe tomorrow we can shop for another bed. I have a second bedroom, but I use it for an office. It should work fine for the time you're here."

He heard the tension threading its way through her voice and desperately wanted to comfort her. But even to touch her would ignite the desire he was struggling against, and if she responded to him with just a flicker of encouragement, he knew they'd be spending the night together in her bed and there'd be no need to buy another for his stay.

It's just a business arrangement. Temporary. You owe her more than a one-night stand. He ground the words into his thoughts, knowing he'd have to obey the rules. He wouldn't allow himself to hurt Darci in that way.

"I'll get some sheets out," she said. She turned and left the room, almost running from his presence.

Cole looked at Scruffy with a rueful grin. "I don't suppose you'd show me where the bathroom is, huh?"

A wheezy snort was his only answer.

Used to unfamiliar places, Cole set the dog down and followed Darci, certain his chances of finding his destination were pretty fair. Instead, he bumped into the very person he wanted to avoid. When he put out his hands to keep her from falling, his fingers settled against her breast, shooting a trail of desire up his arm. He had to fight not to pull her against him, not to explore the tantalizing body hidden under her strictly tailored suit jacket.

Her gasp brought him back to his senses, and he gently set her away. "I'm sorry, are you okay?"

"Fine." Her smile was tight. "I have clean sheets and two blankets. Will that be enough?"

He wanted to answer no, to say that he wouldn't sleep unless her warmth was beside him.

"That's fine. I'm one of those people who doesn't want much tangled around me when I sleep."

She blinked, and he knew she'd read between the lines and pictured him as he slept. He'd never slept in anything but his own skin and couldn't imagine starting to use pajamas now.

"Oh." She hurried on down the hall, and he grinned when he heard the snap of the sheets. The electricity building between them needed to be defused, but he was damned if he knew how to do it. A long, hot night of loving was the only solution he was aware of, and that was impossible.

As he splashed water on his face, he began to wonder what Darci slept in. He could picture her in a proper little nightgown, collar buttoned to the top. When she slept, she'd pull the covers over her head and burrow in like a small rabbit. And he wanted to be the one to slowly peel away the covers, to gently reveal her secrets, until she was open to him, wanting him as badly as he wanted her.

He turned the water to cold and splashed his skin a few more times with little effect.

She was gone when he came out of the bathroom, and he could hear a gentle rustling behind the closed door across from where he stood. The thought of her stripping off that tidy little suit set his blood on fire again, and he sighed, knowing it was going to be one of the longest nights he'd ever spent.

After being up all the night before worrying about Mandy, he should have slept hard. But he couldn't keep all the problems from parading through his thoughts. Mandy, the things he was being forced to do to assure her some sort of future, and Darci.

The few minutes in which he managed to find a comfortable position on the overstuffed couch and actually doze off were interrupted by dream images of Darci. It was with a sigh of relief that he greeted the gray light of dawn. He slipped on his jeans and stumbled into the kitchen to make coffee. He needed it hot, black and . . . now.

As the brew bubbled into his cup, he crossed his arms and stared out the window. The mountains offered him a silent support, reviving an inner strength he was afraid he'd lost.

Cole scrubbed a hand across his forehead, trying to erase the exhaustion hovering over him. He'd have to find time to see Mandy today, have to talk with her doctors and make a decision about a new medication.

He had taken several months off from the rodeo circuit to be with Mandy after the accident. He couldn't stand the thought of being away from her when she was hurting. When she'd finally healed enough, he'd tried to go back to work. But he had been rusty and distracted, a dangerous combination during a rodeo. His horse had gone down, and Cole had spent the next few months trying to heal his own body.

He'd been forced to look for another way to pay the bills. And his only option had been the family company he'd grown up hating. Even in these few short days he needed to set up their future, he'd missed his little girl, missed her forgiving love, her innocent laughter. Very soon, he'd have her with him again.

Darci walked into the room, ruffling her tousled hair and yawning widely. Scruffy trailed in her steps, looking equally sleepy. Darci stopped when she saw him, blinking owlishly. "I thought I smelled coffee."

"You did." With a flourish, he presented her with his cup and set another under the coffeemaker's slow stream. Scruffy settled at his feet, looking hopeful, and Cole almost asked if the dog drank coffee, too.

Darci hugged the cup closer, looking as if she was afraid he would snatch it away from her. Sitting down, she took several sips of coffee in quick succession, closing her eyes in pleasure. "I'm worthless until I've had my first cup. Can't even manage a shower without a shot of caffeine."

She dragged a hand through her hair and peeked up at him. He almost grinned at the thoughts he knew were tripping through her head. She'd let him see her with her guard down, let him view her at her worst. But he thought she looked adorable and resisted a haunting urge to sweep her into his arms and show her another very effective way to wake up.

Her eyes slowly focused on the man standing in her kitchen, and she fought against the flush warming her cheeks. Heavens, this was almost as bad as the morning after, she thought as she shoved a tangle of hair away from her eyes. She always had her first cup of coffee before getting dressed, but it seemed horribly intimate to be sitting here with Cole, neither of them ready to meet the day.

And it seemed unfair that she was experiencing the awkwardness of morning without knowing the pleasures of the night.

Cole had slipped on his jeans, but had left his shirt off, and she had a sudden picture of him sleeping on her couch, nothing covering his skin but the moonlight. Her fingers itched to trace the muscles on his chest, to tangle in the scattering of hair shadowing his skin.

A shaft of fear darted through her as she realized she teetered on the edge of a danger that was all too real. In just two days, she'd let her fantasy love grow and develop until it was becoming a very tangible part of her life.

She squirmed, burying her thoughts in another sip of coffee.

"Darci, we need to talk."

Her head jerked up at the tone in his voice. This wasn't business, of that she was certain. A mixture of warmth and dread curled through her stomach.

"There's something between us that we're going to have to deal with if we expect to work together for the next twelve months."

Eleven months and 29 days, she amended silently, but who was counting?

She gulped another swallow of the strong coffee, hoping desperately for something to rescue her from this conversation. Once they got to the office, it would be okay, she promised herself. She'd be distracted by work, be concentrating on her job, and Cole's magnetic draw would fade into the background.

She hoped.

The man was a temptation she wasn't certain she could resist. It was like being offered ice cream on a blazing hot day. But she was the one who was melting, drifting into a sense of mindless need that was becoming very hard to ignore.

She couldn't allow herself to fall for him, couldn't become any more attached to him than she already was. Because he was going to leave her again. He'd made that clear right from the start of their strange relationship.

She took another gulp of coffee, sloshing the hot brew down the front of her bathrobe. "Ouch!" She brushed at the hot liquid, holding the scalding material away from her skin.

Cole grabbed a towel and knelt in front of her to blot at the stain spreading across her chest. His movements slowed, and his gaze slowly drifted upward to meet hers. The hand holding the towel halted, and she felt the heat of his gaze burn through her.

Her tongue darted out to lick suddenly dry lips, and his eyes carefully watched the slight movement. He leaned a fraction closer, his gaze riveted on her mouth, and she knew she had to stop him. She didn't want to; she needed to feel his mouth against hers again, but she wasn't certain she had the strength to halt what his kiss would surely lead to.

"You're going to leave me, too."

Cole jerked back, his eyes slowly refocusing. With a tortured sigh, he leaned back, still kneeling on the floor in front of her. "Are you all right?"

"I think so. But you're going to leave me, too, aren't you?" She needed to hear him say it again, needed to drill the idea into her head until she was repeating it in her sleep. Maybe then her body would get the message and quit responding to him with such mind-shattering intensity.

He scrubbed a hand over his face. "I have to, Darci."

"Why?"

"Because we made a deal."

"Deals can, and are, broken."

He frowned at her, and she would have given a lot to see into his thoughts at that moment.

"Are you saying you want to rewrite our agreement?" A trace of hope, of longing, flared in his eyes, but it was quickly extinguished. He didn't wait for her answer. "This is what we agreed to, honey." His voice softened as he traced his fingers across her cheek. "Do you want to change that?"

His offer broke through the sensual web he was weaving around her and she stood abruptly, almost knocking him down. "Of course not. I just want to see where we stand with each other. As you said, there is an attraction between us, but I think it's best if we ignore it. We have too much at stake to give in to a brief fling."

She flinched at her own words as she rinsed out her coffee cup. It would never be a fling on her part, couldn't even resemble one. Because her childhood puppy love had developed into something very close to the real thing these past two days.

Her hands gripped the edge of the sink as she stared out at the fading dawn. Blackmore's Gourmet Chocolates. She had to remember her priorities and what was important in her life. The company came first. There was no room in her life for a man, no time to allow anyone else to hurt her.

"Cole, what if we fail? What if the board goes against us?" The words brought a cold chill to her skin, and she rubbed her hands up and down her arms in an attempt to ward it off.

His capable hands settled over her shoulders, and he pulled her back until his hard chest was pressed against her back. She wanted to lean into him, to let him share some of the burden she carried, but she didn't dare. That would bring a new sense of intimacy between them that would only increase their awareness of each other.

"We won't fail, honey. We can't, so we won't."

She couldn't halt her reluctant laugh at his confidence. "You make it sound easy."

"It is. We have five days to plot our strategy. I have some ideas I think will help, and we'll convince the board that it's the only way to go."

His fingers targeted her tense muscles and began slowly working out the kinks. She sighed and closed her eyes, leaning her head against him, letting herself drift with the sensations he stirred inside her. His words were so simple, so basic, she could almost convince herself to believe him.

Her mind wandered. She could get used to this, could become accustomed to his touch, his voice...to him.

The blaring ring of the telephone broke the mood, and Darci jerked away from those tempting hands. Snatching up the receiver, she listened to the voice on the other end, trying to stave off the panic growing inside her. Finally, she nodded her head, forgetting the caller couldn't see her, and blindly set the receiver in its cradle.

"Darci?"

She felt numb, wooden. But she forced herself to look at Cole. He needed to hear the words, to know that all their plans were about to disintegrate. She just didn't want to be the one to tell him. But there was no one else.

"That was Alex."

"Your secretary?" Cole came toward her, grasping her shoulders gently. "What's the matter? What did he say to upset you so much?"

Her numbed mind tried to sort through the words she needed to say. "The board meeting. It's been changed.

The next meeting is tomorrow morning at eight o'clock.''

She sagged against him, needing his strength now more than ever. ''I think we've just run out of time.''

Chapter Six

The day had proved grueling so far. Darci told Alex to cancel all her appointments, then shut herself in her office with a pot of coffee and Cole. The tension still hummed between them, but her entire focus was on the candy-making company her step-father had built and turned over to her with complete faith that she'd make it work.

And now she was about to fail him.

She smoothed her tightly bound hair as she tried to stretch the kinks out of her neck. "This is impossible." Her pencil tapped her irritation out on the desk.

"Nothing is impossible."

She glared at Cole, tired of his positive attitude, tired of his unfailing energy, tired of his total support. There was a strong urge in her to pick a fight with someone, to let off some of the tension building inside her, and he was handy.

"We can't do a year-long work plan, financial projections and all the trimmings by the end of today."

"Do I detect the first notes of a discouraging word?" He shifted until he was sitting on the edge of her desk, his relentless pacing halted for the moment.

"Cole, admit it, we can't work miracles."

Cole leaned across the desk to kiss the tip of her nose. "That's what they want us to think." He tapped his fingertip on the spot he'd just kissed. "They think we'll panic."

"Who's they?"

"Whoever pushed up the date of the board meeting. We were supposed to roll over and play dead, let them have a clear path to present their own ideas."

"And who would that be?" Deep in her heart, she knew the answer, but she wasn't willing to admit it, wasn't willing to acknowledge that her own mother would do anything to have Darci removed from her position as president.

"Who has the most to gain if you step down, Darci?"

"Uncle John, of course." She gulped, forcing herself to face up to her suspicions.

"And who is his primary backer?"

"My mother."

"Why does your mother want you out of here so badly?"

Darci sighed her frustration. "Because she's afraid I'll become an old maid, that I'll never let go of my work long enough to find a man. She wants grandchildren, and she's getting tired of waiting. I think she's decided if she rips the corporation from my hands, I'll get a husband and we'll all live happily ever after."

Darci pressed her lips together, trying to halt the flow of angry words, but she knew she had to say it, to let

Cole know what he was up against. "I've barely had time to date since Daddy got sick. Until she introduced me to Jeffrey. Even then, we didn't go out that much, but by some stroke of unimaginable luck he said he fell in love with me, anyway."

Her laugh held an edge of bitterness. "My mother's promise of a seat in the president's chair was enough incentive for Jeffrey to agree to anything. I can just imagine what a loving relationship we'd have had."

"I'm sorry, honey." He stroked a finger down the side of her cheek, and she resisted the urge to lean into his touch. "They haven't won yet. I've still got my secret weapon."

"If you've got some hidden talent, I could certainly use any brilliant suggestions right now."

Cole glanced at his watch. "It should be arriving any minute now. In fact, I told it to bring lunch. I figured we could work while we eat."

Her stomach growled, reminding her she'd been too distraught to eat breakfast. Both of them had quickly dressed and rushed straight to the office, the awkwardness of waking up in the same house washed away by their worry over the immediate future.

Darci bent toward the papers she'd been sorting. She jumped when a loud war whoop echoed throughout the building. "What on earth?" She stood, prepared to go see what was going on.

Cole slipped a hand around her waist and held her back. "Just wait, honey. The show's only beginning."

The door banged open and a man walked in. Not just any man, but a real live cowboy, complete with spurs on his boots, a bandanna tied around his throat, and an oversize hat shadowing his face. He strutted in like he claimed ownership, grinning at Cole. "You young fool, how the hell are you?'' The man punched Cole in the arm.

"Settle down, old man. This is a place of business, not a rodeo arena." But Cole's grin and his welcome was reflected in his voice.

The man turned to Darci with a jaw-splitting grin. "And just who is this little filly?"

Darci stared at him in disbelief, not certain how to feel about being called a filly, even more uncertain about how to respond to the man who seemed intent on taking over her office. "I should never have let Alex go to lunch," she muttered.

Cole cleared his throat. "My wife. Darci, this is Todd Perkins, the man who's going to help us win the war."

Todd snatched off his hat with a sheepish grin. "I'm pleased to make your acquaintance, ma'am. Sorry about all the racket, but I've been cooped up in the truck too long and needed to let off some steam." He stuck out his hand, pulled it back to examine it, then poked it out again.

Darci hesitantly put her hand in his, relieved when he gave her fingers a gentle squeeze and released her. If this was Cole's secret weapon, they were in bigger trouble than she'd suspected.

"Where's that lunch you promised, Todd?"

"Well, the horse I was going to barbecue got away, so I had to settle for hamburgers." He stepped out of the office and grabbed several fast food paper bags.

Darci felt a laugh bubbling up inside her, suddenly not caring about anything but the wonderful smells wafting toward her. Cole grabbed several napkins, and with a dashing flourish, made three place mats on her desk. He and Todd carefully spread out hamburgers, french fries

and chocolate shakes, arranging everything as if this was
the finest gourmet meal.

Cole stepped behind her and pulled out her desk chair.
"Madam." He swept his arm through the air to indi-
cate she should sit.

When his lips brushed the skin at the back of her neck,
she froze, aware only of the sensations shooting through
her body with lightening speed. When the pleasure quit
zinging around, it settled in the pit of her stomach, stirring up the desire she'd managed to keep buried for most
of the morning. Quickly, she stuffed a french fry in her
mouth, trying to distract herself.

Cole remained behind her, reaching over her shoulder for his own food, and she resisted the urge to turn
around. She wanted to see the expression on his face, to
see if he was as affected by all this as she was. But she
was afraid to, afraid she'd be wrong . . . afraid she'd be
right.

He moved close again, but this time only to speak low
in her ear. "Relax. In spite of appearances, he has one
of the finest business minds I've ever met." His lips
lightly stroked her ear as he spoke, and she almost
choked on her food as she tried to swallow. How could
she relax if Cole insisted on touching her every time he
was near?

Todd grabbed his burger and propped his feet up on
her desk, but Darci was pleased to see he was careful to
keep his spurs away from the polished wood. After he
swallowed a mouthful, he grinned at them both. "Now,
let's get to work. I hear it's the last hand and you're
down and out of aces. Show me what you've got so far
and we'll figure out how to make it work."

Cole briefly outlined what they needed to do, where
they needed to go and how they hoped to do it. Todd

frowned over the papers as he gobbled down his meal, then dropped his feet to the floor with a loud thump and began to pace.

Darci glanced at Cole, but he simply shrugged as he finished his chocolate shake. Suddenly, he leaned forward and traced the rough pad of his fingertip slowly across her upper lip. "You had some chocolate on your mouth."

He leaned away as if nothing had happened and proceeded to pile up their garbage. Darci struggled to pull a breath into her lungs, blaming her light-headedness on lack of air rather than Cole's touch.

Todd stopped and glared out the window. "Okay, here's the plan. We take what you've already done, because you're both definitely on the right track. But we need to expand on it, build it up. You're being way too cautious. You need to spend some money, kids, and it won't be pocket change. Big things come only to those who take the big chances."

"Another famous quote from Todd Perkins himself." Cole finished clearing the desk.

A hesitant knock sounded at the door.

"Darci?" Alex looked in, a confused frown worrying his face. "There's an old saddle under my desk. Is there something I need to be doing with it?"

"Don't touch that, mister. That's my saddle, and I parked it there for safekeeping. Don't trust these big cities, and I don't have a place to lock it up just yet."

Alex looked to Darci for confirmation and she nodded, barely suppressing her grin. "Just move it to the side, Alex. We'll deal with it later."

Alex nodded, cast a suspicious glance at Todd, then backed out of the office. A loud thump echoed through the door, and Darci exchanged a knowing glance with

Cole. But once their gazes locked, she couldn't break away, couldn't force her thoughts back to the problem at hand. The gray of Cole's eyes urged her closer.

Electricity sparked between them, and she found she was becoming addicted to that rush of excitement every time Cole was near. His eyes crinkled, and she lowered her gaze to his mouth, which was turning upward in a tantalizing grin. She licked her own lips and watched that smile fade, watched his mouth thin as if he were trying to gain control over himself.

Todd cleared his throat and the mood was broken. "I know you two are newlyweds and probably don't want to keep your hands off each other, but we do have work to do."

"Our relationship is only a business arrangement, Todd."

Cole's voice held a biting tone that hurt Darci worse than his actual words did. She knew what the terms of their agreement were, but she kept forgetting, kept letting her dreams get in the way of reality.

"Yeah, right. And I'm the good fairy." Todd's words were low, almost muttered to himself, but Darci caught them and wondered if there was something in Cole's look besides desire, something she could hope to build her tomorrows on.

The intercom buzzed, pulling her thoughts once more away from Cole. She was getting tired of all the interruptions, yet they were the only things that were saving her from making a fool of herself. If they were alone in her condo right now, she might well be tempted to seduce Cole, to try to make him love her. Because with each passing moment, she wanted more from him— wanted him to stay in her life, to be by her side through whatever life chose to dish out.

The impossible dream.

The intercom buzzed again, and she forced herself to answer.

"Your mother's on line two."

Darci cringed, knowing that she wasn't going to like the next few minutes. "You gentlemen go ahead with your plotting and scheming. I'll just be a few minutes."

The two men moved to the couch on the other side of the room, and Darci reluctantly picked up the telephone. Her mother's voice sounded without any greeting.

"You'll be expected for dinner at six. We have business matters to discuss."

The words were a royal command, and Darci was expected to obey. A twinge of rebellion almost made Darci say no. She'd been counting on spending some time with Cole this evening, needing to be with him, to torture herself just a little more.

"Cole and I would be delighted to come."

"The invitation was meant only for you, Darci."

Darci recognized the tactic; divide and conquer had always been one of her mother's favorite methods of control. Darci felt the tear of family loyalties again and once more was forced to choose her husband, even if he was only temporary family. "I'm sorry, I won't be able to make it. Cole and I will be working late tonight."

"So you're choosing him over me again?"

Darci tried to push away the guilt her mother's words generated; tried and failed. But Darci refused to play the game to the point of giving in to the demand. She could control that much, at least. "If that's what you're forcing me to do, yes, Mother, I guess I am."

The call was disconnected without any further discussion. Darci held the receiver away from her ear and stared at it, blinking away the tears that insisted on gathering in her eyes. She should be used to her mother's tactics by now, should be able to let the words run off her back like fresh rainwater. But Darci still felt the pain, still wished her mother could just love her daughter as she was instead of trying to manipulate her.

Suddenly Cole was there, his large hands sliding onto her shoulders, offering a casual kind of support. His touch was like a balm to her wounded emotions, and she leaned back, closing her eyes and pretending—pretending he really was hers, that he really did care.

"Trouble?" His voice was soft, coaxing—his hands warm, gentle.

His thumb stroked the side of her neck, and she allowed herself a few seconds to savor his touch. She wanted to believe her fantasy so badly it set off an ache deep in her heart. "Just Mother trying to set us against each other again."

"I'm sorry." He wrapped his arms around her and pulled her back against the solid strength of his chest. His lips caressed her hair as his warm breath stirred her senses.

"I think we're set, guys. You'll wow them at that meeting tomorrow, and it'll be smooth sailing from now on. This plan can't fail once you implement it."

Reluctantly, Darci pulled away from Cole's touch. She was worried about Todd's confidence, but Cole seemed to agree with him, and most of the ideas they'd put on paper were bigger, better versions of her original plan. It should work, it had to work. Because right now, she stood a good chance of losing everything she'd ever wanted in her life.

Blackmore's had meant too much to her for too many years. And now that Cole was insinuating himself into her life, he was becoming too important, too much a part of her. If he could do this in just three short days, she couldn't imagine how she'd feel after their year was up. But then again, if she lost at the meeting tomorrow, Cole would leave sooner and she might still have time to save her heart.

Todd walked over and gave her a gentle punch on the arm. "Knock 'em dead, kid." He turned to Cole. "Dude, we need to talk. You got an office where we can meet for a few minutes?" Todd stretched, wincing as he moved. "This old cowboy's got to find a place to crash. I drove most of the night to get here, and the old body's starting to complain."

"Todd, why don't you stay with us tonight? There's no sense in renting a motel room when I've got plenty of space." Darci knew her offer was selfishly motivated. With Todd there to act as a buffer, maybe she could keep from making a fool of herself over Cole.

"I don't think there's room for both of us on that couch, Darci." Cole grinned at her, taking the edge off his words.

"I'll get a bed ordered for the spare room and have it delivered this afternoon, okay?" Pink stained her cheeks. Talk about sleeping, beds and another night alone in Cole's company stirred up sensations she was desperately trying to ignore.

"I don't want to put you out none, young lady. I can find a dive to stay in that won't cost much."

"Nonsense. Both of you be there in time for a late dinner." With her words, she knew she needed Todd to break the awful tension building between her and Cole, knew she wasn't strong enough to resist the temptation he offered much longer.

Todd nodded his agreement and stepped to the door. Cole stood several feet away from her, eyeing her carefully. Just before he turned away, he softly whispered, "Chicken." Without another word, he left.

When he closed the door behind him, her office, the room she'd always felt so complete in, became empty, lifeless—as if Cole had taken all the energy with him. Darci sat in her chair with a heavy sigh. It was already happening. Maybe it was too late to save herself. Her heart was falling in love with Cole without her permission.

And Cole was right. She was chicken.

Cole hurried down the hallway, feeling like he'd barely managed to escape with his sanity intact. What had possessed him to play with Darci like that, to allow himself to taste her sweet skin, to touch her soft lips? It was crazy. He'd never allowed himself to tease a woman, had never played the sex games the other cowboys seemed to indulge in. After his wife had died, Mandy had taken every ounce of his concentration and energy.

He greeted his secretary with only half his attention, and darted into his new office. With a sigh, he flopped into the leather executive chair and leaned his head back to stare at the tiled ceiling. He desperately wanted to make love to his new wife. It was legally his right, but he had his suspicions about the morality of such an act since theirs wasn't a real marriage.

He couldn't pursue what he so desperately wanted because of a rash promise made when other things seemed more important. Darci called to him, sending out a siren's song he was finding more and more difficult to resist.

He had to stay away from her, had to quit allowing himself to touch her, to kiss her...to fantasize about her. The only other choice was to take her to his bed.

Todd sauntered into the room, and Cole let his wants go with a sigh of relief. He had to concentrate on Mandy, on just getting through each day. It was the only thing that could possibly keep him from breaking his promise to Darci.

As the heat in his body subsided, he agreed with the wisdom of having Todd stay at the condo. With a guest there, neither of them would be tempted to pursue the need building between them. Cole couldn't help but wonder how he'd survive when Todd left.

"Wooee! That secretary of yours sure has a temper. I just tried to pay the little lady a compliment and her claws came out." Todd patted his chest with a frown. "I think I escaped with all my skin intact."

Cole shook his head, not daring to imagine what his friend believed was a compliment. "Behave yourself, Todd. I have to work with the woman, so don't antagonize her. Just this once, try to resist your natural urges."

Todd grinned. "But they're part of my irresistible charm." He dragged a chair up to the desk and sat down. "How's my little darlin' doin'?"

Cole dragged a hand across his face. "Better, but not well enough to come home yet."

Todd nodded. "What happens now?"

Cole hesitated, not certain how to answer. But he'd talked through many problems with Todd and knew that any rambling discussion might get him pointed in the right direction. "Somehow, I'll have to talk to Darci, explain about Mandy."

"You haven't told your wife about Mandy?"

"I didn't tell Darci when we agreed to marry, and now I can't quite figure out how to bring it up." Cole glared at the ceiling. "My mind was so focused on getting control of the company, I didn't think through all the details." Cole leaned his head back with a tired sigh, wishing Todd could provide some magic answers. "This marriage is only a temporary arrangement, and I can't let Mandy and Darci get too attached to each other, but how can I possibly keep them apart?"

Todd frowned. "You plan to have them live in the same house together, but not get too friendly?"

Cole winced. "Sounds impossible, doesn't it? And maybe it is, maybe I'm busily destroying everyone around me. Maybe I haven't a chance of salvaging my life. But I can't quit trying, either."

Silence filled the room as Cole let his mind run through all the moments he'd spent with Darci these past few days.

"She wants family, Todd. Home, hearth and all the trimmings. She wants something I can't give her."

"Why not? There's certainly sparks flying between you two. And where there's sparks, there's fire. You could stay in Denver." Todd's face lit up as he began to plan Cole's life for him.

"Your rodeo career is probably over, and you don't want to be one of those hangers-on everyone just feels sorry for. Take the chance, Cole. Stay married, start a new family, try to make the relationship and the company work. You could build something for the both of you, and I think Darci really loves you, even if she won't admit it." Todd grinned. "Have you seen her eyes when she thinks you're not looking?"

Cole resisted the urge to tell his friend that if he wasn't looking, he wouldn't be able to see her eyes. But he could imagine them, the green of her eyes deepening with the desire he'd stirred in her this morning. Just the memory set off a slow burn deep in his gut.

Todd stood, turning his hat in his hands. "You got problems, that's for sure. I'm just an out-of-work cowboy, but you've got yourself a tangle that may never get straightened out. But you know I'll help any way I can." He jammed the dusty old hat on his head. "I got some chores to do. Should I meet you back here later?"

Cole agreed, shook hands with his buddy and walked him to the hallway. Cole didn't want to take the chance of Todd irritating his secretary again.

He stood in the hallway, staring into the emptiness. He'd have to talk with Darci...and Mandy, would have to try to prepare them for what would come in the future. Somehow, he'd have to find the right words, make them both understand. The two women in his life were both desperate for love, looking for attachments, and he had to find a way to keep either of them from getting hurt when he was forced to leave Darci.

Or else he'd have to pick up the pieces when it was all over. And he wasn't certain he had the strength to do that again.

"Mr. Blackmore?"

He turned away from his troubles and forced his attention to what his secretary was saying.

"The hospital's on the phone, sir. Shall I put the call through to your office?"

Cole nodded, his skin going cold as he hurried to the phone. If anything had happened to Mandy, he'd never be able to live with himself. Deep in his heart, he knew he was doing the best he could, but he couldn't convince himself it was enough, couldn't believe he didn't have the ability to work miracles.

"Hello!"

The nurse's soft voice assured him Mandy was fine, but that she was asking for him.

"Tell her I'll be there shortly." Hang the business. He'd explain to Darci later. Right now, he was going to his daughter, and no one, not even a stampeding herd of wild buffalo, could stop him.

When Cole's secretary informed Darci that he wasn't in his office, Darci set the receiver down with a frown. Once again, he'd disappeared without an explanation, had walked out on his obligations to her and the company. Anger simmered inside her. He'd made promises, vowed to do whatever necessary to help her win this battle. But he was of no help to her if he continued to run off at the whim of the wind.

She glared at the phone and wondered. Was it possible Cole was no better than her natural father? As much as she had loved the man, even her six-year-old mind had seen him for the irresponsible wanderer he was. And one day, his wanderings had taken him out of her reach. She'd never seen nor heard from him again.

To this day, she didn't know what had happened to him. She only knew he'd left her feeling alone, empty, unloved. Much the same way she was feeling about Cole leaving without saying a word to her.

She wanted, needed, to believe in him, but was beginning to doubt even she could conjure up that much trust when he was proving to be so unreliable.

Alex stepped into her office to ask if she needed anything else, then said good-night, ordering her to get a good night's sleep for a change. Darci answered him with a tired smile, noisily shuffling papers on her desk so he'd think she was desperately busy and leave.

As soon as the door closed behind her secretary, she leaned back with a sigh of relief. She knew she should just give up and go home, relax with a glass of wine, soft music and some wonderful pasta. But Cole would be there, and that would end any chance of relaxing. Besides, right now, she was just too tired to get out of the chair. Maybe if she closed her eyes for a moment, it would revive her enough to make it to the other side of town.

But instead of a quick rest, she drifted off to sleep, images of Cole Blackmore becoming tangled with her dreams. She remembered his touch, his kiss. Her dreams wove the possibilities through her thoughts, making her wish for a future for the two of them. When the dream became more erotic, she squirmed in her chair.

Hands touched her face, stroked her skin. Lips brushed against hers, tasting, teasing. With a low moan, she arched closer to the warm movement, wanting, needing more from the man who called himself her husband.

"I knew you wanted me."

The voice was deep, thick with suppressed passion.

But it wasn't Cole's.

Chapter Seven

"Jeffrey!"

Her dream shattered as she scooted out of the chair, away from his touch. "What are you doing here?" Wiping the back of her hand across her mouth, she pushed her desk chair between them, hoping to ward off any further advances.

His eyes gleaming with determination, Jeffrey reached for her again, but she nudged the chair forward just enough to discourage him. The sweetness of her dream quickly faded, to be replaced by the harshness of Jeffrey's duplicity.

"Come on, Darci. Let's kiss and make up. Let's go back to the way it was between us."

His tone was low, coaxing, but she knew she'd never respond to it again. Never the way she did to Cole, to his voice, to his touch.

"I'm married, Jeffrey." She shook her head in frustration when he didn't respond. "Go away. Just leave me alone."

Jeffrey frowned, then leaned on the edge of the desk. Darci couldn't help remembering how Cole's black jeans had stretched taut when he had sat on the very same corner, how her breath had caught just at the thought of his strong muscles pressed against her. In comparison, Jeffrey seemed overpolished, almost soft in his carefully pressed business suit.

"I just wanted a chance to talk with you without the toy cowboy around."

"Trust me, he's no toy," she muttered. Louder, she added, "He's my husband, Jeffrey." Holding up her left hand, she wiggled her ring finger to confirm her words. "Love, honor and cherish, till death do us part. I'm sure you've heard the words somewhere before." She'd heard the words, had listened and wished with all her heart they were true, that Cole could stay with her forever. But some dreams simply weren't meant to come true.

When Jeffrey didn't respond to her reminder, she sighed, knowing he didn't choose to acknowledge her wedding vows. "I don't want you here in my office. Please leave."

"We can still get your... contract with the cowboy annulled, Darci. We can still be married to each other. I do love you, and I know you love me."

She shook her head at his ability to forget what he'd done to her. "You love my corporation. A man who truly loved me wouldn't take another woman to his bed just after he became engaged." With a touch of surprise, she realized that the pain of his betrayal had faded, just another sign of how wrong her engagement to Jeffrey had been—another sign of how right her marriage to Cole was beginning to feel.

Jeffrey shrugged, showing just how indifferent he was to the entire affair. "I was just letting off some steam, sowing the last of my wild oats."

"I guess you'll just have to keep sowing for a while, Jeffrey. I don't love you and I have no intention of marrying you." She didn't know whether to laugh or cry at her own words. Here she was talking to one man about marriage while already married to another. And neither man wanted her for anything resembling love.

"You're making a big mistake. You know without my help, without your mother's backing, you stand to lose everything. Your daddy's precious company will be taken from your control at the meeting tomorrow."

The suspicions she'd harbored for months finally coalesced into a very real fear. "How did you know about the meeting change?"

Jeffrey simply smiled. "I have my sources. And I have my own influences." He stood, carefully pulling the creases of his trousers straight. "Think about it. Use all that business knowledge your stepfather taught you. You have everything to lose and nothing to gain if you stay with the cowboy."

His words had the vague sound of a threat. Pausing, he watched her carefully, but she refused to react, refused to let him see just how much he'd thrown her. She just wanted to get home to Cole, to have him hold her and reassure her.

"You know where to reach me if you change your mind tonight. We can go into the meeting together tomorrow and set everything straight. By next week, I'll make my mark by pulling your little business out of its slump."

Anger wiped away all the other emotions. "You're awfully confident, Jeffrey. Do you know something I don't?"

He just smiled and walked out the door.

She wanted to chase after him, to shake the truth from him, but she knew he would only laugh at her. Darci eased into her chair slowly, her fingers massaging the tension from her forehead.

She had taken a terrible chance by marrying Cole, but if given the same choice tomorrow, she'd do it all over again. The teenaged boy who had carried a pesky tag-along piggyback down a rocky trail wouldn't deceive her, wouldn't betray her trust. And the man he'd become wouldn't, either. She had to believe that, had to cling to that trust.

And she could never forgive Jeffrey for what he'd done, never forgive him for not loving her at least enough to be faithful to her. She'd known from the beginning of their engagement that it wasn't the wild, passionate love of her dreams, but she'd thought it would be enough, had thought a warm affection would sustain her through all the years to follow.

Now that she'd been exposed to an older, more experienced version of the Cole she'd fantasized about for so long, she realized just how naive she'd been. She needed passion in her life, needed love. But it was becoming an elusive wish that kept slipping through her fingers each time she got close enough to touch it.

The sounds of traffic in the street below finally brought her back to the present. She needed to get home and put together something for dinner. And she needed to see Cole, to touch him and remind herself that he did care for her. He would never love her, but he did care. And that would have to be enough for now. It was all that had been offered to her.

* * *

Her gray eyes pleaded with him, and Cole was reminded of a puppy begging to be loved. His heart clenched as he pulled his five-year-old daughter into his arms and held her close. Somehow, he had to find the magic words, words that would tell her of his love while still explaining why he had to leave her alone again tonight.

"Please, Daddy. I'll be good, I'll do all my exercises and I won't complain."

Cole closed his eyes against the anguish raging through him. "I know you'll be good. You're always good as gold. And I promise you can come home with me before the weekend. I need to set up a bed for you and get the exercise equipment in place. Besides, the doctor says you have to stay here at least one more day until they get your medication adjusted."

A single tear slipped down Mandy's cheek. "I miss you, Daddy. I hate this place, and I'm lonely."

Cole wiped away the moisture on her face, smoothing her hair with his calloused hand. "I miss you too, Snugglebug. So much, it hurts, right here." He put his hand over his heart, knowing it would take a miracle to soothe the pain he carried there. "Just be patient one more day."

The doctor came in, his white coat flapping behind him like an errant child. "How's my favorite patient today?"

Mandy burrowed her head closer to Cole's chest and held him tightly.

"She's a little homesick. Is there any chance I could take her home tonight?" He knew the timing was terrible, but he'd make it work. Darci would understand— maybe too much.

"And take the light out of my evening rounds?" The doctor shook his head. "I'm sorry, honey. I need you to stay with me through tomorrow so I can make sure everything is fine. We don't want to make you sick again, do we?"

"No." Her voice was muffled, but Cole felt the wobble of emotion in that short word, felt it deep inside where it tore at him.

"Good girl." Before he left, the doctor checked the chart and gave Mandy orders to eat all her dinner.

Cole moved closer, pulling her tighter against his chest, wanting to shield her from all the pain, all the uncertainty, but he didn't know how. He was a mere mortal, a man who'd tried and failed. And he could never make up for all that Mandy had lost in her young life already.

But he could share Darci with her, maybe bring a little bit of sunshine into Mandy's life. It would be impossible to keep them apart, but maybe if he said everything just right, he could keep them from being more than friends. Cole stroked his daughter's hair. "I have something to tell you."

She looked up, the total trust in her eyes twisting his insides a little tighter.

"I got married." Her eyes brightened with excitement, and he hurried his words, trying to set things right, hoping there was a possibility her five-year-old mind would understand something he didn't. "It's only temporary, for just a year."

"So I can have a mommy again?"

Cole felt the tears building behind his eyelids and squeezed his eyes closed against the pressure. "No, sweety. She won't be your mommy. It's a business arrangement, just something we did to save the company

I own part of. Once the business is strong again, we'll go our separate ways."

"So you're going to fire her?" Mandy's forehead was wrinkled in confusion.

At her logic, Cole felt amusement squeeze through his pain. "Not exactly. We're just staying together, kind of like playing house while we sort out the business side of things. Then it'll be just you and me again."

"But she can be my friend?"

"If you want her to, yes, she can be your friend." Cole hoped his words were true, and he knew he'd have to find a chance to explain to Darci, to warn her what Mandy expected, what the little girl wanted. Then maybe Darci could help him protect his daughter against any more emotional traumas.

Mandy burrowed against his chest once more. "I'd like to have a mommy again."

He hadn't thought he could feel any deeper, but her words sliced through him, leaving a gaping hole he didn't have a clue how to fill. "I know, Snugglebug. I know." Images of Darci drifted through his mind, but he shoved them away, knowing he was dreaming the impossible. He didn't dare take the chance.

Mandy lay in his arms silently, clinging to him as if she was afraid he'd disappear. Cole struggled with what he knew had to be done. It was time for Mandy to come home with him. He wasn't willing to be separated from her any longer. And Mandy needed him to be close by, to reassure her, to let her know he wasn't going to leave her. But by letting Mandy and Darci get to know each other, he would complicate an already tangled mess of a marriage.

Mandy had barely gotten over the loss of her mother, and she was desperately looking for another woman in her life, a woman she could call mother and give all the love little girls held in store for their parents. Cole loved his daughter more than life itself, but he sensed that wasn't enough, knew deep down that perhaps Mandy's battered body needed more love than he had to give.

Darci was another shattered soul looking for that elusive thing called love. She'd told him of her need for children, he'd seen her caring ways when she was a young girl. Mandy would bring out all Darci's mothering instincts. If he wasn't careful, he knew he'd end up hurting the two most important people in his life. And yet, all he really wanted to do was help everyone, do what was best and not hurt any of them.

Hell.

He'd managed to make a royal mess of his life.

The lights were on when she unlocked her door, and she halted, savoring the sense of someone besides Scruffy being there to greet her. Her dog darted into the room, his tail wagging his entire body.

Someday, she hoped to have a child running to greet her. Someday when she had a real marriage. She tried to imagine another man in her life, a different face moving close to hers for a welcoming kiss, but failed. It was Cole's kiss she wanted, Cole being there to greet her. Forcing away the disturbing thought, she bent to pet the squirming bundle at her feet. Until the right man came along, Scruffy, the poor little mop, would get all her attention, all of her love.

When Cole stepped out of the kitchen, she stopped scratching Scruffy's stomach and stood, letting her senses absorb the tall, dark man standing in her living room. He looked tired, the lines around his eyes reflecting a fatigue as bone deep as hers. But he still managed a smile of greeting and held out a glass of wine for her.

Her fingers closed around the stem, his hand brushing over hers as he pulled away. She couldn't resist smiling into his gray eyes as he leaned forward and pressed a gentle kiss of greeting on her lips. Warmth wound its way through her stomach, reminding her of all she was missing.

"Welcome home, honey. I was beginning to think I'd have to send out a search party."

His scent, his touch, flooded through her, washing away the last remnants of Jeffrey's kiss. The memories of deceit that had haunted her on the drive home melted away, too.

"I...uh...got tied up at the office. Let me just change clothes and I'll find something for us to eat."

He stopped her with a gentle hand on her shoulder. "Relax. Dinner is taken care of." A loud bang came from the kitchen. "By the way, thanks for inviting Todd to stay. I can't do enough favors to return what I owe him."

She shrugged. "I couldn't let him go to some cheap hotel after all the time he gave us."

Cole's grin sparked a small flame inside her.

"He has more money than he could ever spend, so don't feel too sorry for him."

Darci raised her eyebrows in doubt.

"He just chooses not to spend it." Cole nudged her toward the hallway. "Go change, enjoy your wine and come to the table when you're ready."

She hadn't gotten more than three steps before she stopped again. "Where were you this afternoon?" She winced as the words slipped out, couldn't believe how much like an accusing wife she sounded.

"I had some urgent business." He grasped her shoulders, forcing her to stay when she tried to turn away to hide the hurt his words had inflicted. "Business that we'll discuss tomorrow after the board meeting. You have enough on your mind right now without adding my problems to your plate."

She opened her mouth to protest, but he tightened his grip, halting her argument.

"Darci, you need to relax tonight, prepare your thoughts for tomorrow. Everything else can wait."

Silently, she nodded, showing him her agreement. But when he released her, she watched him cross the room with a deep frown between her eyebrows, wondering if he was just like Jeffrey, if Cole didn't see the need for keeping vows, either. She couldn't help remembering the times he'd disappeared without explanation.

If he'd cheated on her already, she wasn't certain she'd survive. Because unlike her relationship with Jeffrey, Darci knew she loved Cole, deeply, with a lifetime commitment that would be dashed to bits at the end of their first year together.

That was the agreement. She had no choice but to play by the rules.

And if she didn't tell him about the incident at the office, she'd be guilty of something almost as bad as cheating. She wanted fidelity and trust from Cole, and she owed him the same thing. She owed him her honesty.

"Cole."

He stopped and turned, waiting for her to speak.

"I'm late because Jeffrey came by the office."

Anger darkened Cole's features.

"Somehow, he's in on all this. He wanted me to annul my marriage to you and stand by his side at the meeting tomorrow."

"Did he touch you?" Cole's arms were held rigidly at his sides, his hands clenched.

She shuddered deep inside. "He kissed me."

"And you just let him?"

The words were almost toneless, no accusation was reflected in his voice. But Darci felt herself getting angry, anyway. She shouldn't have to defend herself. "I'd fallen asleep at my desk and he let himself in. I didn't wake up until it was too late."

Cole nodded, acknowledging her words, but not releasing the anger she could see building inside him. His warning about locking her office door hovered between them, but Cole had the good sense not to remind her.

Finally, he spoke. "I guess he didn't take my warnings seriously. I'll have to make myself clearer the next time we talk."

"We gonna rumble with someone?" Todd came out of the kitchen, a white apron tied around his waist and a big wooden spoon clutched in one hand.

Cole gave him a tight smile. "Just a little personal matter that needs my attention."

Todd looked disappointed. "Haven't had a good fight in months." He turned to Darci with a smile. "Get that city-slicker suit off, young lady. Your dinner's about cooked and I'm starved."

Darci saluted him with her wine glass, anxious for an excuse to escape Cole. He was too angry, and she wanted him too badly. A few moments of privacy might give her a chance to get her defenses back in place.

Comfortable and secure in her jeans and an old sweatshirt, she joined the men in the kitchen, looking for a harmless topic. "So, Todd, you're also a master chef?"

"I'm just an old cowboy who likes to eat. Cole did the cooking, I'm doing the stirring."

She turned to look at Cole, trying to hide the amusement tugging at the corners of her mouth. "When you lived at home, you could barely pour yourself a glass of water. What happened?"

"I got hungry," he said simply. Tasting the chili boiling on the stove, he added more spices and turned away from her. But she wasn't going to let him get away that easily. The need to tease him, to lighten the tension between them, was irresistible.

"And it's edible?"

"This boy's chili's won contests all over the West. It'll steam your sinuses and put hair on your chest." Todd's already ruddy cheeks deepened in color, and he muttered, "Or whatever it does for you gals."

Cole laughed. "Stuck your foot in it again, huh, Todd?"

"Shut your mouth, boy, and serve dinner before I eat it all right here."

Fragrant bowls of chili were dished up and served with corn bread so perfect Darci made a quick check around the kitchen to look for mix boxes. Not finding any evidence, she shook her head in disbelief, then hurried to the table to eat before everything disappeared.

Her first bite of the spicy concoction brought tears to her eyes, but she eagerly ate the entire bowlful. "This is wonderful, Cole. You'll have to give me the recipe."

"No recipe. A little of this, a little of that, whatever's in the fridge, and you've got chili. Turns out different every time."

Darci watched Cole finish his meal, wondering at the different sides of him she was getting to know. She'd been hoping that as they spent more time together, she'd find out he wasn't the man of her dreams. Unfortunately, the more she learned about him, the deeper her love grew.

It was supposed to be the other way around. She was supposed to discover Cole really was the lazy, shiftless wanderer his father had always portrayed. It would have been much easier on her that way, much simpler to walk away when the time came.

Todd soaked up the last of his chili with a piece of corn bread. "So when can I expect to be an uncle?"

Darci choked on the sip of water she'd just taken. Cole leaned over to thump her back while he glared at Todd. Longing knifed through her as she struggled to control her coughing. She wanted children, a large family, to whom she could give all the love she'd been harboring for too many years. She wanted to have the chance at the warm family life she'd missed in her own childhood.

"I thought I'd explained this wasn't that kind of marriage." Cole's voice was tight.

"You did, I just don't choose to believe it. You two kids belong together, but you're too stubborn to see what's right in front of you."

Cole grabbed his dishes and carried them to the kitchen, his posture tense. "You're wrong, but I'll never get you to admit such a thing, will I?"

Todd winked at Darci. "I'm never wrong and he knows it. I'll be back to help you celebrate your first wedding anniversary, and I'll expect to be invited to the baby's christening."

Warmth flowed through her veins, finally pooling deep in her stomach. To have Cole's children, to be able to give him all her love, was a dream she'd barely dared to recognize. But now that Todd had put it into words, the thought had been firmly planted in her mind, and Darci knew it was what she really wanted.

Blackmore's Gourmet Chocolates was like her baby now, demanding all her energy and attention, but children would easily take its place. If she lost both her job and Cole, she wasn't certain she'd be able to force herself out of bed each morning. And she wasn't certain she'd be able to build another relationship with another man, pinning her hopes and dreams on a faceless partner somewhere in her future.

Cole was the only man she wanted.

Trying to run from the pain her thoughts were generating, she grabbed her own dishes. Cole had already put away the leftovers and was washing the kettle.

"I can do that." She set down her dishes. "You cooked, I should clean up." She needed action, activity of any kind to distract her thoughts.

"Is that another one of those rules of marriage?" He rinsed the soap off the oversize kettle.

His work-roughened hands drew her attention. "No, but it's the fair way to do things."

"And you always play fair, don't you? No matter what the cost?"

She suspected his words held a deeper meaning, but she was too tired to sort them out. Instead, she slipped her dishes in the dishwasher and turned away. She had to get away from him, had to put their relationship back in its proper place. "I'm going to take a bath."

He stopped her retreat with a hand on her arm. "Darci, I'm sorry. It's been a hell of a day, and I'm taking it out on you."

She frowned, waiting for him to share what was eating him alive. She sensed there was something else in his life, something deeply disturbing. But she had no right to demand answers, to probe deeper. If she were a real wife, she could gently lead him to talk about it, but in their present situation, she felt it was up to him to make the first moves toward revealing his secrets.

His fingers cupped her face, and he smoothed away the frown on her forehead with his thumb. "Don't, honey. Don't waste your worry on me. I'm not worth it."

"Yes, you are. You're worth it to me." She hadn't meant to say the words, hadn't wanted even to hint at her growing love, but now that the words were out, she was glad. Maybe he would see the love she offered, change his mind and stay with her after all. She'd dreamed bigger dreams and had them come true.

"Sweet Darci."

His mouth closed over hers, the first delicate touch becoming deeper, stronger, as his hands roamed over her back. When his tongue brushed against her lips, asking for entry into her mouth, she opened to him, savoring the taste and texture that was so uniquely Cole. Almost frantic in her need to learn his secrets, her hands swept over his arms, then around his neck to tangle in his hair.

He moaned deep in his throat, the sound vibrating through her and setting off an answering moan. Pulling her closer, he tucked her between his legs so she was left with no doubt about her effect on him. His hands stroked a path to the sides of her breasts, teasing and tantalizing until she wanted to pull him to the kitchen floor and show him just how much she really loved him, how much she needed him.

But the sound of someone gently clearing his throat stopped her from making her wants reality. Cole reluctantly pulled away, leaning his forehead against hers while his breath dragged raggedly through his lungs.

"If you two are done 'washing the dishes,' I'm thinking about getting me some sleep. Where do I get to bunk down for the night?"

"Oh, no, the bed." Darci almost moaned again, but in frustration this time. Her body was on fire for Cole, but she couldn't allow anything more to happen. "I forgot to order a new bed."

The temptation was there to suggest Cole simply sleep with her, as was his right as her legal husband. But she knew the emotional toll would be more than she could survive. She knew deep in her heart that once she had him, she'd never want to let him go. Watching him leave would be difficult enough without adding the burden of a physical bonding.

"I don't suppose I can share yours tonight?" His whispered words brushed against her face, renewing the memory of his touch.

Heat coursed through her. She gulped and forced out the word that needed to be said. "No."

Cole grinned, his tight lips at odds with the amusement in his eyes. "I didn't think so."

He stepped away, and she felt the loss of his warmth.

"You get the couch, Todd. I'll make do with the floor tonight."

"Cole, no."

He turned to watch her carefully with those gray eyes, eyes that reminded her of a brewing storm. "I've slept in worse places. Just give me a couple of blankets and I'll be fine.''

The house grew quiet with an ease that was surprising considering the tensions simmering in the air. She curled up in her own bed, snuggling Scruffy close, feeling guilty for making Cole sleep on the floor. But there was no other choice. At least not for her.

After chasing the elusive escape of sleep for several hours, Darci gave up. Scruffy grunted his protest when she finally climbed out of bed. Slipping on her pink satin bathrobe, she padded into the kitchen, opening the curtains on the bay window that looked out over the Rocky Mountains visible from her backyard. She waited for the scene to soothe her as it always did—waited in vain. For the first time, her life was totally out of her control.

She would make her pitch in the morning, lay it all on the line, but after that, her future was in the hands of six men. All six had sat on her stepfather's board of directors, all six had honored her stepfather's wishes and let her remain in the presidency. Until now. There had been more and more rumblings of discontent these past few months, no doubt fueled by frequent urgings from Uncle John.

If given the time and the freedom to make needed changes, she was certain she could turn the profit curve around. But the board had constantly stalled her efforts for change. She'd talked to each member over the past two weeks, tried to convince them to side with her, tried to show them that Blackmore's needed to move into the nineties. But she had no way of knowing whether she was having any effect. Tomorrow would decide everything.

Including the state of her very unstable marriage.

"Worrying won't change anything."

Cole's deep voice sifted over her skin. Refusing to turn, she continued her vigil at the window. "I know that, but my mind has other ideas."

His fingers curled around her shoulders, offering his strength and comfort. "Everything looks much worse after midnight. When the sun comes up, your entire perspective will change."

"Promise?" She needed to believe him, wanted to just let it all go.

"I wish I could, honey."

She twisted in his arms, laying her head against his bare chest, the warmth and scent of his skin giving her something else to think about.

"Cole, I'm so scared." She leaned into him, letting him offer comfort, taking the strength he so willingly shared. The doubts, the fears, no longer mattered. When his arms were around her, she knew she loved enough for both of them, knew that she could make him happy. Blindly, she turned her face toward his, offering her lips.

After only a second of hesitation, he brought his mouth closer, their breath mingling, his warmth teasing her. Ever so slowly, he fitted his mouth over hers, sending a volcano of sensation shooting up deep inside her. She wanted to cry out against the sweet agony, but the only sound that escaped her lips was a low moan.

He pulled her closer, tracing his fingers over her skin, seeking out secret places she longed to have him touch. Desperate to return his touch, she traced the muscles of his shoulders.

"I love you."

When he slowly pulled away, she realized she'd whispered the words against his lips. The stark light reflected in his eyes told her all she needed to know, and she felt the first crack in her heart, knowing it was one of many she'd have to endure in the future.

"Don't become too attached to me, honey. I'll just break your heart."

But as he turned away, she knew it was too late. He already had.

Chapter Eight

The rain beat against the window, sending Cole's mood into even blacker depths. He glared at the area where he knew the mountains stood watch, but the peaks were covered with heavy clouds. He glared and remembered—her soft mouth moving against his, her warm body pressed close, her scent, her touch—memories that still held the power to arouse him hours later.

Against his will, a thought crept through his head. He was falling in love with Darci. For the first time in his life, he was faced with a love that could last forever. What he'd felt for Sharon had grown into a deep friendship, but he'd never been able to return the love his first wife felt for him.

But Darci was different. Cole closed his eyes against the force of his feelings.

He never should have let things between them get so hot last night. Because now, even with the cold light of day staring at him, he wanted her more than ever. But he couldn't allow himself to have her—he wouldn't take the chance of anything happening to Darci.

Glancing at the wall clock, he went to the phone, knowing he didn't dare forget another promise. Mandy was counting on his call, and he was going to assure her he would get her out of that hospital this afternoon, no matter what. He wanted to be with his daughter again. And he needed her undemanding love around him. It was the only thing that had saved his sanity these past months and he was counting on it carrying him through the difficult times yet to come.

He waited impatiently for the phone system to connect him to his daughter's room. Finally, he heard her voice and his mood lifted a little. ''Hi, Snugglebug. How's my girl today?''

''Can I come home now?''

A reluctant smile tugged at his mouth. ''This afternoon. I've got a business meeting this morning, then I'll come straight over to break you out of that place.''

She giggled, just as he'd intended. ''Do I get a saw baked in a cake?''

''You've been watching too much television again. I might be talked into bringing that cake, but don't worry about breaking a tooth. I have a better way of getting you out.''

''I miss you, Daddy.''

He leaned his head against the cool kitchen wall, letting visions of Mandy dance through his head. Without warning, Darci joined his daughter in his mind, and the two shared their laughter. To have the three of them together, as a real family, was something he wanted so badly he could almost touch the images.

''I miss you, too. Eat all your breakfast and I'll be there as soon as I can.''

"I love you, Daddy."

Her words wrapped around him, warming the coldness surrounding his heart.

"I love you, too." His voice was raspy with emotion. Blindly, he replaced the receiver. He was doing the only thing he could do. But was he going to destroy Darci in order to save Mandy?

"Rough night?"

Cole jerked away from the wall and stared at Darci, the words to call off their arrangement hovering on the tip of his tongue.

He forced a smile to his stiff lips. "Yeah. I spent a lot of time thinking about the board meeting." *And you,* he added silently. The dreams he'd woven while lying on his makeshift bed had destroyed any chance of sleep. He'd finally drifted into a troubled sleep toward dawn, but when he woke, the desire was knife-edged, threatening to sever him in half with the wanting.

"I spent a lot of time thinking, too."

She traced her fingers across his forehead, brushing back a wayward curl. He could see the reluctance in her eyes when she pulled away, and he almost reached out to pull her close and give her a good-morning kiss, allowing himself to taste her mouth once more, to share her warmth. But he knew even that simple act would lead to more than either of them were ready to handle.

"Breakfast?" Darci filled the coffee maker as he watched her movements, mesmerized by her gracefulness.

"Just coffee."

"I'm too nervous to eat." The unspoken possibilities hung in the air between them. "Maybe we can have a big celebration lunch."

Positive words wouldn't hurt, but Cole had his doubts about them being any help, either.

"You look nice today." The compliment seemed too mild, too bland, for what she did to him. Her tailored red suit made her look every inch the businesswoman, her cream-colored blouse underneath the only feminine touch in her look. But that trim coolness made him want her even more, made him want to shatter her control again, to watch the need slip into her eyes.

Her smile held a faint tremble, and he wanted to reassure her. But he was so afraid his promises weren't worth the breath it took to say them.

"I can't believe you really slept on that floor all night, boy." Todd came into the room, his hair still rumpled with sleep, a long flannel nightshirt hanging around his knees.

"Where else would I sleep?" Cole regretted the question as it escaped.

Todd raised one eyebrow and glared at him. "With your wife, maybe?"

Cole just shook his head, giving up on the effort of convincing Todd about the facts of their marriage. When Cole stepped across the room to pull down several coffee mugs, he noticed the faint blush on Darci's cheeks. He couldn't resist reaching out to trace the pink tinge, and his touch raised her color another notch.

He smiled, satisfied that at least she was as frustrated as he was. It was a small consolation, but he knew he wasn't trapped alone in this tangle of unfulfilled desire.

"After the meeting, there's someone special I want you to meet." Darci tossed a questioning glance at him, but didn't pursue her curiosity.

"You mean you're finally going—"

For once Todd was silenced with a glare. He snorted his disgust, grabbed a cup of coffee with a mumbled thanks and headed for the shower.

Cole poured himself a cup of coffee and turned away from the woman he wanted more than the air he needed to breathe. "I'll be ready to go in a few minutes. Or as soon as I can pry Todd from the shower."

"Cole."

The hesitant quality of her voice made him pause, almost dread to turn around.

"I'm going to leave for the office now. Do you think Todd could drop you by when you're ready to come in?"

He struggled against the feeling of being shut out, knowing that wasn't Darci's intention. "I guess so, yeah."

"I...need to be in my office alone for a while. Hopefully it will help me collect my thoughts before the board meets."

His gut wrenched, and he wished he could make everything work out for her, wave his magic wand or something. "Are you sure?"

She looked at him, her green eyes stormy, troubled. "I need to prepare myself for any possibility."

He could see it in her eyes. She needed time to say goodbye, to let go of her legacy. "Darci, don't."

"I have to, Cole. You know as well as I do that the odds are against us. The board wanted to remove me as president at their last quarterly meeting, but I convinced them to give me a little more time."

"How can they expect you to work miracles if they don't allow you to change anything?" He clutched the mug so tightly he was afraid it would shatter. Maybe that would be good, maybe it would release something in him, something that wanted to knock some sense into someone.

Her smile was tired, drawn. "I'll see you at the office." She moved to step past him.

He halted her, searching her face for something, anything. With his thumb, he gently smoothed the dark circles under her eyes. "You haven't gotten much sleep since I've barged into your life, have you."

She simply shook her head and walked out, leaving him to wallow in his own doubts.

Todd dropped Cole off in front of the office building. "You be good to that little gal, boy. Stay with her and she'll make things right for you."

"I've told you—"

"I know, it's only a business arrangement, but I can see different with my own eyes. It's time to start a new life. Make yourselves a baby, and everything will turn out as the good Lord intended it to."

Cole winced, but Todd drove off before he could answer. Todd was on his way to another rodeo, the dust and sweat as much a part of him as breathing. The old man would die while chasing the next rodeo, but he'd die happy. Cole, on the other hand, wasn't even certain how to make himself happy. But he knew that keeping Darci in his life would be a good start.

If only he could.

Cole hesitated at Alex's desk. The two of them hadn't managed to establish any kind of working relationship. Alex didn't completely trust Cole, and Cole wasn't ready to give his respect to Alex.

Alex was the first one to break the silence. "I think she probably needs your support right now. Go on in."

Cole nodded his thanks and opened the door.

Darci stood with her back to him, arms crossed, staring out the window at the gray sky overhead. The distant mountains were shuttered in the gray fog, adding to the dreary tone of the morning.

He closed the door, searching for the right words. "I'd like to say this is where I came in, but it was better before I arrived, wasn't it?"

She didn't turn around. "Not really. I've been on the verge of losing it all for months. I just keep thinking I can pull a rabbit out of my hat and it will all be fine again."

"It's not over yet. Don't give up hope." He winced at the inane words, but had nothing else to give her except false reassurances. They'd talked yesterday about the odds of their success, and they both knew the future was balanced on a very fine thread, a thread that could break at any time.

The only thing in their favor was that they controlled a large share of stock. The board was supposed to take their wishes into consideration before each vote. But that was like wishing that all politicians were honest. If all the other shareholders voted against them, they would still be outnumbered.

Darci had spent part of yesterday afternoon calling some of the directors she trusted, but none of them were willing to give her their total support without seeing what she had to offer. None of them trusted the girl they'd watched grow up, none of them had accepted the fact that she was a woman now, an adult capable of running a large corporation if they'd only give her a chance.

Darci finally faced him. "Well, there's no sense in delaying this any longer. Let's do it."

They entered the boardroom together, carefully timing it so they were the last ones inside. Cole closed the door, then joined Darci at the table. She stood at the head of the room, opening the meeting with a casual greeting as if she were seeing old friends.

Cole sat at her right side, Alex on her left. The two men exchanged glances, and Cole suddenly knew that Alex would help Darci in any way he could. Unfortunately, as an executive assistant, his power was limited.

Her presentation was thoughtful, professional and calmly presented. Cole felt pride swell in his chest as he watched her work. She knew what she was doing. But then he looked around the room, saw the doubt on the board members' faces. And he knew the first cold brush of fear. They weren't listening, weren't willing to take the chance. The entire room was closed to the concept of change.

He wanted to stand, to demand they really give her a chance, but he didn't dare antagonize them. Darci had suggested she do all the talking since the board knew her, and he'd agreed. His only claim to the company was a distant relationship with his father and a large portion of stock. These people had no reason to believe anything he said.

Cole forced his attention back to Darci's words. There was still a chance, the vote hadn't been taken yet.

"We need to move into the future, stay on the cutting edge of the technology. I realize this will take money we can ill afford to spend right now, but I think the risk will pay off in the end."

Darci turned to the charts she and Cole had spent so much time on yesterday. "We need to change our packaging, try new marketing techniques and build a new niche for ourselves. The old way of doing things isn't reaching this generation of buyers."

Darci braced her hands on the table and looked at each board member. "All I'm asking for is the opportunity to try. Give me your trust to do what needs to be done and I'll turn this company around in one year. If at the end of that time I haven't accomplished what I've promised, I'll relinquish the presidency without a fight."

One board member spoke up. "But by that time it may be too late to save anything. Our cash flow is low enough that it would take every penny we have in reserve to make the changes you're suggesting. We have a responsibility to the shareholders, and we can't allow you to take chances that have no possibility of succeeding."

"My proof is here." Darci pointed again to the charts and graphs. "It will work or I wouldn't suggest it. You seem to forget that this company is my legacy from my stepfather. I wouldn't do anything to harm it. I only want to see success for our future."

Cole resisted the urge to applaud her words.

"Darci, we need more. To take this big of a risk, we need guarantees."

"No one can give you a guarantee, Mr. Webber." Darci directed her words to the senior member of the board. "But you can see the statistics for yourself. If we continue at the present rate, we'll be bankrupt within one year. And unless we make some changes, this downward trend isn't going to turn around."

"What has happened is simply a result of a downturned economy. That's changing now. Our figures will go up, just like the economy, if we're just patient."

"I don't agree."

The ring of authority in Darci's voice made Mr. Webber sit up straighter. A frown of doubt settled between his eyebrows, and Cole felt his first stirrings of hope since the meeting had started. Another man started scribbling madly on a piece of paper, muttering over a set of numbers only he could possibly understand.

Somehow, she was getting through to them; maybe, just possibly, there was a chance.

"And Mr. Blackmore would be joining the company as a vice president?"

"When you appointed me to the presidency, you gave me all the authority that comes with that position. I chose Mr. Blackmore because he's very qualified to fill the position. He brings us a new perspective. In fact, he's invested as much time on this new plan as I have."

She cast a slight smile toward Cole, and he suddenly felt like he could do anything and win.

"You two were married just this week."

"Yes."

"And you both received additional shares of stock on the day of your marriage."

"That was in my stepfather's will, yes. Both of his children were to receive additional shares when they married."

"There was no stipulation that you marry each other?"

A frown gathered between Darci's eyebrows. "I don't think anyone considered that possibility."

"So this isn't a love match. It's just a business arrangement." Mr. Webber didn't even have the grace to look uncomfortable with his question.

"I don't think that's any of your business." Her words held a cold edge.

"Anything that affects this company is my business. Do you love each other?"

Darci didn't look away from her tormentor, didn't even blink. "Yes, we do."

Cole released the breath he'd been holding through the last several questions. He knew the show they'd begun had to continue, but he didn't want Darci to be forced to lie, either. Unfortunately, there was little choice in the matter. This group was unwilling to accept their authority based on marriage only. They wanted to see a total commitment, or they wouldn't believe the couple was devoted to the business.

Mr. Webber studied Darci carefully as the seconds ticked slowly by. Cole wanted to do something, anything, that would add weight to Darci's claim. Not certain what he had to say, he stood.

"Excuse me, but I feel I need to add a few words here."

He waited as all faces turned to him, a myriad of emotions reflected by the different attendees. Darci slowly sat back down, and he wasn't certain what her feelings were about his speaking. But he couldn't remain silent any longer, couldn't let these men doubt Darci's abilities based on her relationship with him.

"Darci has run this company for several years now. You should all know that she's good at what she does, and she should have been offered your trust to do what's best for the corporation years ago."

Cole paused, waiting for his words to soak in. "The basis of our marriage has nothing to do with our ability to do what needs to be done. Darci has an intimate knowledge of this company that you'll find hard to match anywhere. And even though I've been just a rodeo cowboy, that still requires solid business practices that I think will be an asset to Darci."

He spread his hands, offering what little he could to reassure the board. "We both care about Blackmore's Gourmet Chocolates, both want to see it prosper. And I think, if you'll just give us a chance, we can make this work to benefit everyone involved.''

Cole sat down to total silence, a hushed expectancy that never developed.

Finally, Mr. Webber nodded, breaking the building tension. ''We'll adjourn this meeting while the board considers all the options. Return in an hour and we'll give you our final decision.''

Anita Blackmore stood. ''I feel I should have a chance to present an option to the board.''

''That's fair. What did you have in mind?'' Mr. Webber turned to watch Darci's mother.

''I would like to suggest bringing in some new blood. Darci has had her opportunity to show what she can do and it's only gotten us into trouble. John and I have been looking for a capable man and would like to recommend Jeffrey Simms as the new president of this company.''

Darci gasped, the blood draining from her face. Cole reached out to her, weaving his fingers through hers as he tried to transmit some of his strength to her. He wanted to stand up and call Anita the liar she was, but he knew that would only hurt their cause. What he needed to do was figure out what Anita was up to and why. They should have done more investigating into Anita's motives. There was something deeper here, something too complex to be sorted out at the last moment.

''Is Mr. Simms here now?''

''Yes, he's been waiting in Darci's office. Would you care to talk with him now?''

Cole fought with his anger as Darci's fingers clenched his with a tight grip. She was distraught, but he wanted to hurt someone. Simms was probably already planning how he was going to remodel the office to suit his needs.

Mr. Webber frowned at the other board members, and they all nodded in reluctant agreement.

"If you'll excuse us, we'd like to interview Mr. Simms."

Cole followed Darci into the hallway, proud of her dignified carriage. She wasn't going to let them see how desperately she wanted to win. And he knew from all his years in competition that looking like a winner was often part of the battle.

Darci went to the water cooler, poured herself a drink and gulped it down. She reached for another cup, filled it and handed it to Cole. "What do you think?"

"They're a hard bunch. They're all too old, too set in their ways, to do this company any good."

Sighing, she leaned against the wall. "They won't even accept the responsibility for putting us in this position. I've wanted to make these changes for two years, but they've stalled me at every turn. I wish I could buy them all out."

"If we robbed the bank on the corner, we could make a cash offer right now." She needed to smile, and he was rewarded with a slight turn of her lips.

"Don't tempt me."

Mr. Webber looked around the corner and motioned them back to the board room.

"That was fast." Cole rested his fingers in the small of Darci's back. "Too fast."

Darci didn't even acknowledge his words, but he could feel the tremors sliding through her.

Mr. Webber droned on about statistics, the national economy and business in the Denver area in general.

Cole felt like a child trying to sit still in church. Finally, the older man looked up, his features grim.

"Mr. Blackmore, we'd like to speak with Mrs. Blackmore alone for a moment."

Cole wanted to refuse, wanted to stay and protect her from the world, but he knew that was beyond his limited powers. Reluctantly, he stood.

Hesitating, he stopped beside her and, on impulse, pressed a quick kiss on her lips. Let the board think whatever they wanted; he didn't care anymore. He simply wanted to offer Darci his support and couldn't think of a better way to do it.

Darci's mother gasped at the display and Jeffrey frowned.

The chairman of the board turned to Anita Blackmore and asked her to leave also. Jeffrey followed in her wake like a well-trained collie.

Unable to think of a reason to delay, Cole finally turned away from Darci, silently sending her all the strength he could. Her face had gone white, yet she stood seemingly calm while her future was about to be decided by six old men with little understanding for what she was trying to accomplish.

It was only a few minutes, but each second that clicked by seemed like an eternity to Cole. He prowled the hallway outside the boardroom, determined to be the first person to approach Darci when she came out—either to congratulate her or console her.

Everything was out of his hands now. He'd played his cards, gambled with two lives, and it was all on the table. He could only hope for the best.

When the boardroom door opened, he turned, his heart ceasing its relentless beat until he saw Darci. Her set features, her white face, told him more than any words.

They'd lost the war.

He clenched his hands at his side, forcing himself to go to her, to pull her into his arms. Silently, he held her, feeling the tremors race through her. When she raised her head, he could see the pain, the sense of betrayal, reflected in her eyes.

"They've asked me to step down so Uncle John can take over until they have a chance to investigate Jeffrey as a possible candidate." Her voice was a bare thread of sound. "I didn't really believe they would do it. Why, Cole?"

His own troubles were roughly pushed aside by her anguish. It was happening again. He'd let himself get close, had allowed himself to care, and now he was being forced to watch as she was slowly, methodically destroyed.

Anita stepped into his view. "I told you, Darci. I tried to warn you, to protect you from this, but you refused to listen. Now you have nothing but a washed-up, out-of-work cowboy for a husband and no job for yourself."

Darci leaned her forehead against Cole's shoulder, her body limp and unresisting.

"I think that's enough for now, Anita."

"Yes, Cole, I'm sure you do. But you're the cause of this disaster. If Darci had just done as she was supposed to, she'd be happily married to Jeffrey and the company would be in good hands."

"Somehow I doubt she'd be any happier." Cole couldn't keep the bitterness from his voice. "But you always did know what was best for everyone, didn't you."

Something flickered in the older woman's eyes, and Cole almost dared to name it regret. But there were too many angry words between them, too much distance, for him to offer her a way out now.

"Why does it matter to you, Anita? What do you care what Darci does? She was happy doing this job, was breaking her neck to keep your dividend checks rolling in so you could enjoy the life-style you've become accustomed to."

Anita Blackmore straightened, glaring her hatred at Cole. "I hate this company. It took my husband away from me. I never saw him, and the long hours eventually killed him." A shudder rippled through her. "Then I lost my daughter to the same corporate monster. All I could see was her devoting her entire life to a pile of concrete. I wanted her to be happy, to have the family she's always dreamed about. But she didn't even have the time to date."

Anita's voice shook with the strength of her emotions. "I want to see this company destroyed. And Jeffrey is just the man to do it."

Darci finally looked up, her eyes haunted by her mother's words. "He knew what you wanted?"

"He knew, and he was to be well rewarded for his efforts."

Darci shook her head, confused by her mother's logic. "How would he be rewarded? Your bread and butter would be defunct, and we'd all be looking for work."

"I have money put away. Enough to keep Jeffrey happy and by your side, and enough to keep me living comfortably. Jeffrey and I even had plans to start a new enterprise, something that you wouldn't be interested in."

"I don't think you truly understand how much money your plans would take, Anita." Cole tamped down the anger building inside him. The woman's logic was so badly skewed he couldn't even come up with a decent argument.

"I understand more than anyone has ever given me credit for. If you had just stayed away, Cole, it would have worked. You may have managed to ruin part of my plan, but I'll still be rid of this company." Her voice dropped to a threatening whisper. "And there's nothing you can do to stop me."

Cole wrapped his arm around Darci's shoulders and pulled her into the hallway. "We'll be in my office."

"You don't have an office, Cole. Your position has been terminated as of now," Anita said.

"Until I hear that from the new president of this company, I'll be in my office." He kept walking, refusing to acknowledge Anita's sputtering protests.

He fixed Darci a cup of coffee, seated her in his leather chair and held her hand. When she didn't respond, the panic began to creep through him. If only he'd stayed away. If only he'd looked for another way to save himself. Instead, he'd managed to drag her down with him. He could go back to the board, demand to be heard and expose Anita's plans. But, it was doubtful they would listen, even more doubtful they would believe him.

Pushing the guilt aside, he tried to get through to her. "At least this means we won't have to work this weekend."

She didn't respond.

"I hear the weather's supposed to be perfect, so we'll have to plan something special."

She blinked, but still didn't acknowledge him.

"Darci."

Finally, she looked up at him. "I still can't convince myself that they really did it. I thought we had a chance. We never did, did we? The decision was already made before we even got here."

The wounded disbelief in her voice caused his hand to tremble as he smoothed a stray curl away from her face. "I think you might be right. But we've still got almost a year left of our agreement. We'll just have to find another way to save the ranch."

Did he dare consider staying with her for the agreed-upon year? Would fate find a way to tear her life apart even more if he hung around? Would he be able to resist her potent draw?

One corner of her mouth tipped into the beginnings of a smile. "This was my entire life, Cole. All my plans have centered around Blackmore's for as long as I can remember. Now I have to start all over, and I don't even know where to begin." She sighed, her shoulders finally slumping with her defeat. "I have no source of income, very little savings and no job prospects. Know anyone who'll hire an out-of-work company president?"

"I would if I could, honey. But defunct rodeo champions don't have much better prospects."

Knowing there was one thing that would take her mind off her troubles, he stood, tugging gently on her hand. He would share the light of his life, and hopefully manage to bring a smile to Darci's eyes again. "So we'll just forget about it all until next week. Come on, honey. I have a surprise for you."

Hand in hand, they stepped into the hallway. They walked past the people congregated outside the boardroom, ignoring everyone. Together, they turned into her office so she could pick up her purse. Just as they stepped inside the plush room, the sun broke through the clouds, casting a glow on the furnishings. Cole couldn't help hoping that for once this was a good sign, hoping that somehow, some way, he'd fix everything that had gone wrong.

But he still hadn't mastered the art of working miracles.

Chapter Nine

Darci glanced around her office, her *former* office, barely seeing the furniture that had served during her stepfather's reign as president. The effects of total defeat numbed her emotions. She hadn't thought the board would replace her, had honestly believed she and Cole stood a reasonable chance of winning.

Too unnerved to indulge herself with the release offered by anger or tears, she simply stood by the desk, waiting for something, anything, to break through her shattered emotions. Several years of her life had been focused on what this room represented, but nothing here really belonged to her.

With an odd sense of detachment, she picked up her nameplate, grabbed her purse and turned to face Cole. "I'm finished, let's get out of here."

"That's all you're taking?"

"Yeah, I guess so." She went out into the front office, not noticing whether Cole was following or not.

"Alex, thanks." She held out her hand.

Alex's jaw hardened. "I don't think—"

"Please, don't. Just wish me luck. I hate goodbyes."

He finally put his hand in hers and squeezed her fingers gently. "Good luck, Darci. Maybe now you can get caught up on your sleep." He turned to Cole. "Take care of her, she's special."

"I know." Cole's hand settled at the small of her back.

She heard Cole's words, but couldn't dredge up any response to his approval. Her world had just been ripped out from under her, and she felt like she was in a free fall with no chance of finding a parachute. And she had no clue what to expect when she hit the ground.

"Do you want lunch?" Cole took her keys from her limp fingers and guided her to the passenger seat of her car.

Willing to let him take charge until she could make her brain work again, Darci shook her head, trying to force all her concentration on the traffic swirling around her. If she took the next few days one minute at a time, she just might stand a chance of surviving.

When the car stopped, she looked around in confusion. "What are we doing at the hospital?"

Cole shifted in the seat, then raised his gaze to meet hers. The hesitation, the fear, the doubt, were all reflected in his eyes. "There's someone here I'd like you to meet."

Searching for answers, but coming up with nothing that made sense, Darci frowned, waiting silently for him to explain.

His gaze slipped away from hers, and he stared blindly across the parking lot. "I have a daughter, a beautiful five-year-old girl named Mandy."

The words fell into her thoughts, but Darci had to repeat them to herself several times before they made sense. The news articles she'd collected had never mentioned a daughter.

Unexpectedly, anger washed through her, replacing the numbness she'd been fighting. "You have a daughter and you never bothered to share that detail with your wife?"

Cole had the good sense to look uncomfortable. "It was probably the wrong way to approach things, but it seemed like a good idea at the time."

"Trust me, it wasn't." Her heart ached as she realized that Cole had never meant to include her in his life, had never considered that they could build something permanent. She tried to blink away the angry tears building in her eyes. He'd deliberately withheld a vital part of his life from her. "And just how long did you think you could keep her hidden from me?"

"Just until she got out of the hospital."

Darci felt her mouth open, wanted to berate him, but the words halted in her throat. She finally managed to swallow. "She's in this hospital?"

Cole nodded.

The anger faded away as Darci finally realized why he'd disappeared without warning, why he seemed distracted at odd moments. Reaching out, she tried to offer comfort as sympathy flooded through her, replacing the sense of betrayal. "I'm so sorry. Tell me about her."

"Seven months ago, my first wife was killed in a car accident. Mandy..." His voice cracked on the word and he swallowed hard. "Mandy was badly injured in the wreck, but she survived. She can't walk unaided right now, but after months of operations and physical therapy, it's just a matter of building up her muscles again.

In fact, she graduated to crutches just last week, and the doctor thinks she'll be walking by herself soon."

Her fingers tightened on his arm. With a rush of blessed feeling, Darci realized how trivial her troubles were. She was alive—young, healthy—and she could start over.

Quicker than she'd thought possible, a new determination swept through her—a determination to succeed, to build a new life for herself, a life without the controls and strictures the company and her mother had smothered her with.

But right now, Cole needed her. She'd give him as much time as he wanted, then set out to rebuild her life. With fresh determination, she focused her attention on Cole. For the remainder of the afternoon, she resolved not to think about Blackmore's.

Cole caught her gaze, held it, almost pleaded for her understanding. "I promised her she could come home today. And I'd like you to meet her."

"Why didn't you tell me about her before?"

Cole squeezed his eyes closed and sucked a deep breath into his lungs. "Mandy's desperately looking for someone to love, for another mother. I can't afford to let you two become too attached to each other, because we both know this is a temporary arrangement at best." The apology sounded in his voice. "I was trying to figure out how to keep the two women in my life safe and happy. I thought if I just had enough time, if I stalled the inevitable, I'd find the magic answer."

"I understand, Cole." Her heart ached for what could have been. All three of them were looking for that elusive thing called love. All three of them were just waiting for the right person to come along, but it never seemed to happen. "Let's not make her wait a minute longer."

He looked at her again.

"I'm hurt, Cole. You should have trusted me. But our contract didn't say anything about getting involved in each other's personal lives. And I would very much like to meet her." Darci reached out, resting her fingers on his forearm. "She can stay with us at the condo until we sort out everything that's happened and decide where we, and this marriage, go from here."

His lips tilted upward in a grim thank you.

When they entered the quiet hallways of the hospital, Darci sought out Cole's hand and tangled her fingers with his. As they waited for the elevator, he stared at their intertwined fingers without comment.

Darci knew she was probably giving something away that she'd rather keep secret, but he needed her right now. And her hand was all she had left to offer.

They stepped into a small room and a squeal of delight greeted Cole. "Daddy, you came!"

Breaking free from Darci, Cole strode forward, pulled his daughter into his arms and held her tightly. It was at that moment Darci was certain of something she'd been fighting since Cole walked back into her life. She would willingly stand by this man's side no matter what the world chose to dish out to test them. The sweet puppy love of her teenage years had grown into a lifetime commitment.

He'd proved himself so many times these past few days, had stood with her and supported her through it all. Suddenly, the final traces of the pain left by Jeffrey's betrayal, of her mother's manipulations, were washed away.

With Cole by her side, none of it mattered anymore. With his loyalty to his daughter, Cole had demonstrated his ability to stand by those he loved. And Darci was anxious to meet the little girl, to get to know this small part of Cole who was bouncing happily on the bed.

"Do we get to leave right now?"

"First there's someone I'd like you to meet. Mandy, this is Darci, the lady I told you about."

Mandy sobered, watching Darci come closer.

"Hi. I'll bet you're eager to get outside again, aren't you?" Darci perched on the edge of the bed, achingly aware of Cole's lean strength mere inches away.

Mandy nodded her head, then gifted Darci with a shy little smile. "Are you coming home with us, too?"

Home. Darci had to bite her lip to keep from giving her true feelings completely away. Home was such a small word. And it didn't take much to make one—just people you truly loved and cared about, no matter what. That freely given love was something Darci had never experienced, something she'd always wanted, badly.

"You'll be staying with me for a while. Is that okay?"

Mandy nodded, then held out her arms to Cole. "I want to leave. Now."

Cole grinned and lifted Mandy into his arms.

While Cole dealt with the endless paperwork, Darci combed Mandy's hair into a ponytail, then helped her get dressed. The little girl insisted on wearing jeans, boots and a fringed western shirt. Darci's heart melted with each moment that passed, her hopes and dreams for a family of her own becoming tangled with Mandy's chatter about everything she wanted to do now that she was with her daddy again.

"Ah, my little cowgirl is back." Cole stood in the doorway, his hat tilted slightly to shade his eyes. But

Darci could hear the wistfulness in his voice, could understand his anguish over his daughter's pain.

When the nurse wheeled Mandy to the hospital entrance in the wheelchair, the girl pretended to be riding a pony.

"She's going to grow up to be just like her daddy."

Cole's mouth tightened. "That's what she wants. I just hope I can give it to her."

Darci wanted to help him raise Mandy, but knew she was dreaming the impossible. Cole had made it clear from the beginning that he didn't love her. There was no reason left for him to remain married to her.

Fresh depression settled over Darci as she realized she'd lost so much more than her life's work. Cole possessed her heart, and she wasn't certain she had the strength to take it back again.

She was silent when they drove away, letting Mandy's chatter wash over her.

"Daddy, look, a Ferris wheel." Mandy pointed to a small parking-lot carnival, her nose pressed against the car window.

"Snugglebug, I don't think you're ready for that just yet."

"Please, Daddy. Just one ride. Then I'll take a nap. I promise."

Darci could see him weakening. She knew she should help him, should say something to discourage Mandy, but suddenly Darci wanted that Ferris wheel ride as much as the little girl. It would be one memory of Cole, a special moment that she could savor in the lonely years ahead. She caught his gaze and knew he saw the eager agreement in her own eyes.

Without another word, he turned into the parking lot. Rather than fight with the crutches on the crowded, uneven ground, he lifted Mandy into his arms and headed for the ticket booth. When he stopped, he turned to Darci with an odd expression.

"I don't have any cash with me."

Darci laughed, something she hadn't thought she'd be able to do again so soon. "Well, I do. I should probably save it for groceries or some other important detail like that, but right now, I'm not certain I care." She stepped forward, then turned back to Cole. "How many rides do we want to take?"

"Ten," Mandy called out.

"I think one turn will be plenty," Cole answered with an indulgent grin.

The parking lot was hot, dirty and smelled strongly from all the machinery working around them. Harsh noises filled the air and the crowd jostled them. But when they stepped up to the Ferris wheel, the negative images faded away, leaving only the magic of a shared moment. The lights became brighter and the music sweeter.

Trying to steady the swinging seat, Darci helped Cole settle Mandy between them. Mandy squealed when they slowly started to ascend, and Cole slipped his arm behind his daughter. But his fingers tangled in Darci's hair, settling at the nape of her neck. The rush as they circled higher, combined with the silky stroke of his touch, caused her stomach to swirl with a heady excitement.

Mandy giggled and wiggled like an excited puppy, pointing out everything from blackened rooftops to escaped balloons. Darci's heart filled with the moment, knowing this was a magical time she would never forget. Determined to savor every precious second, she gave her worries over to the clouds above them and simply enjoyed the ride.

When they settled back to earth for the final time, she hesitated before stepping down. She didn't want to leave, didn't want to give up the magic. But it was a moment she could reach back into her mind for when the going got rough, and she knew she could relive it any time she needed to.

Cole helped Darci off the wobbling step, then scooped Mandy into his arms. He swirled around with the giggling girl held tightly against his chest. Mandy's laughter mingled with Cole's, and Darci knew she'd found everything she'd ever wanted in life—a strong man to love and a beautiful child to cherish as her very own.

But she also knew she couldn't keep any of it.

As they walked back to her car, she couldn't hold back the words any longer. "Cole, what happens to us?"

He tucked Mandy into the middle of the front seat, buckled her seat belt, then turned to Darci. He ran the back of his fingers across her cheek, and she resisted the urge to curl into his touch. "I don't know. I guess we need to find some time to talk, to make some plans."

That was something she wasn't certain she was prepared for. She'd rather just drift along for a time, pretend they were a perfect little family, before they made any decisions. But she also knew that would only make the final parting twice as difficult.

She sat beside Mandy, breathing in the little-girl scent of baby shampoo and sweetness. Unable to resist, Darci stroked Mandy's hair, savoring the softness. "What would you like for dinner tonight, young lady?"

Without hesitation, Mandy grinned. "Pizza."

Darci laughed, knowing the sound wasn't as carefree as it should be. "Pizza it is."

Cole slid into the driver's seat and looked at the two of them. "Let me guess. We're plotting the biggest pizza party ever, right?"

Cole gently teased Mandy all the way back to the condo, alternately bribing her and threatening her with no food to get her to agree to do her exercises.

When they entered the condo, Mandy gave a squeal of delight at the sight of a dog, the noise sending Scruffy to hide under the coffee table. Cole knelt on the floor, balancing Mandy on his knee while he coaxed the dog closer. When Scruffy was within reach, Cole scooped the dog up and held him close while Mandy petted him.

"Scruffy hated Jeffrey." Darci had thought her words wouldn't be heard, but Cole looked up and understanding passed between them. He smiled with his lips, but the happiness never reached his eyes.

Darci left them in the living room while she went to order the pizza. It seemed odd to be planning a celebration dinner of sorts after all that had happened today. She should be upset, devastated, but all she wanted to do was have a party celebrating having Cole in her life and Mandy out of the hospital.

The day had been a seesaw of emotions and tangled incidents that would take days to sort through. In the meantime, Darci was determined to set it all aside and enjoy what little time she had with two very special people.

When she got off the phone, she stood in the doorway and watched Cole work with Mandy. The little girl lay on the floor while Cole's big hands guided her through her exercises. His patience was endless, but then he'd always been that way about something he truly cared about. When he was a teenager, she'd watched him work horses before he'd left home, and he'd exhibited the same endless patience then, too.

When Mandy began to whine, he teased her into trying just a little harder, then gave her a big hug and kiss for succeeding. They cuddled together, their heads close as they shared secrets and plans Darci wanted to be included in. Her heart ached as she realized she was an outsider to their love. She wanted so desperately to be a part of it, to share in that warmth, to make their very own little family.

When the pizza arrived, Darci was thankful for the reprieve from her thoughts. Any reason for their hasty marriage was now over, and as hard as she tried, she couldn't come up with any excuse to keep Cole by her side. But she knew she had to make some effort. She wasn't ready to lose him yet. Her heart demanded more time, just a little longer.

Mandy chattered constantly through the meal, but began to wind down as her tummy filled up. When she drooped in her chair, Cole lifted her into his arms and took her into the bathroom to help her get ready for bed.

After she was tucked in on the couch, Mandy protested that she wasn't really sleepy. Darci offered to play a movie for her, knowing the little girl wouldn't manage to stay awake long once she was quiet. Darci slipped a Disney movie into the VCR, then gave in to the urge and kissed Mandy on the forehead before reluctantly returning to where Cole was seated, turning a cup of coffee around in little circles.

The pizza box and paper plates still littered the table, but Darci knew they couldn't delay their talk any longer. Her heart was aching with the effort she was making not to let herself care too much about the two extra people staying in her home. It would be so easy, create so much happiness for three very lonely people, if they found a way to stay together.

But Cole didn't love her.

Her hands insisted on picking up the plates, needing something to distract her from what she knew was coming. She wasn't ready, didn't want to let Cole and Mandy go yet. But there was nothing to hold them here, nothing to allow her to keep them.

"You can stay here for as long as you need. Maybe if we brainstormed, we could come up with a new business to start together. We still have a year left on our agreement; we could use the time to settle into another life." The words tumbled from her lips. She tried to halt them, but they insisted on being said. "I have a little money saved, enough to get us by for a while."

Suddenly, she felt like she was begging for his attention, pleading for his love. Clamping her mouth closed, she stuffed all the garbage into the pizza box and jammed it closed.

Cole reached for her hand, but when she pulled away, he dropped his arm on the table. "I have nothing to offer you, nothing but a truckload of problems that aren't yours. Mandy's medical bills will take me years to pay off. And I won't live off your money. I need to find a way to support myself."

"But what if—"

He cut off her words with a sharp motion of his hand. "It wouldn't work, Darci. We both need to start over, but in different places. I've got Mandy to worry about first, then I've got to think about a new career."

"I could help you with Mandy."

Cole shook his head, and Darci felt her heart twist painfully. "I can't let you give everything up for me."

"I don't have anything left to give up." She regretted the words as soon as she said them, seeing the pain she'd inflicted on Cole.

He glanced up, the past haunting his eyes. "I tried to love my first wife, but I never felt anything more for her than affection."

She winced, then sagged into a chair, not certain she wanted to hear what he had to say.

"Sharon and I made a mistake, and we had to get married because she was pregnant. I tried to be a good husband, but I was too busy, too set on making it to the top to see how lonely she was. Being the wife of a rodeo bum is hard enough, but she wanted me to spend time with her. And time was something I couldn't spare without losing the momentum in my career." He gulped. "She also wanted me to love her."

He picked up a clean napkin and slowly tore it into small pieces. "When she couldn't take the loneliness anymore, she left and took Mandy with her." Cole's hands stopped their relentless destruction, and he swallowed hard. "She hadn't gone two miles when she wandered across the yellow line into the path of a semi. She was blinded by tears, tears that she was crying because of me."

When he raised his gaze to Darci, she gasped with the intensity of the agony he transmitted to her. It was almost more than she could bear to hold his look, to try to offer some form of comfort.

"I destroy everyone I touch. I can't do that to you, Darci. I care about you too much."

The air left her lungs in a rush. The battle was over before it had even begun. Just when she was beginning to think she had something to fight for, that there might be a family in this world for her to love, it was snatched away from her eager fingers.

She didn't have the strength to battle Cole's ghosts. At least not now, not yet. First she had to find her own life, get her feet on the ground; then she could take a chance at salvaging Cole's.

"So it's over, then. This must be the shortest marriage in history." She didn't laugh, but grabbed the garbage and went into the kitchen before the tears hovering in her eyes could slip down her cheeks.

Cole watched her walk away from him, watched her leave with dreams he hadn't even had time to form yet. In his first marriage, they'd both been too young, too immature to truly understand what made a marriage work. And he'd never been able to love Sharon the way a man should love his wife. He now knew he hadn't truly understood what love could be until he'd spent time with Darci.

Deep down, he knew Darci had something special to offer him, that he needed her in ways he'd never needed another human being before. Darci offered him a salvation he wasn't certain he deserved—but at what price? What price would she be forced to pay for caring about him? He had nothing to offer her except a growing stack of medical bills.

When she came back to the table, he had resigned himself to what he needed to do. "We'll leave in the morning. I want Mandy to get a good night's sleep before we start out."

Darci fidgeted with the edge of the tablecloth. "Do you need any money?"

He almost laughed, the bitterness over his financial state overwhelming his already-tattered emotions. "I've got enough to get us where we're going and to keep us fed until I find another job.''

"Where are you going?"

"To a friend's. We can stay there, and I can work for our keep on his ranch." He breathed a sigh of relief when she didn't question him further. He didn't want to tell her where he'd be, didn't want to chance her coming back into his life and tempting him again. Because it wouldn't take much for him to throw caution to the wind and take the chance of loving her. His resolve was growing weaker with each passing minute.

She nodded. "I guess this is it, then. Thanks for trying, Cole. You did everything possible, but we just weren't good enough."

Her lips pressed together, she held out her hand and he glared at it. He wanted to kiss her, to taste her sweet mouth once more, to savor her body pressed against his. But there was no sense in torturing himself again. He'd pretend to go to sleep, spend all night thinking about her, then walk out of her life without a backward glance. It was the only way he could save her.

Not responding to her offered handshake, he stalked into the kitchen, trying to drown his frustration by gulping a glass of cold water. It didn't work.

He glanced around the cheerful room, suddenly feeling trapped. He couldn't stay another night, couldn't take the chance of weakening. Mandy would sleep just as well in the truck and he could drive all night. It was better than staring at the ceiling for hours while he wrestled between the right and the wrong of his life.

Returning to the living room to tell Darci his decision, he froze when he saw her seated on the couch beside his daughter. Mandy was sleeping, and Darci was watching her with a naked longing that tore at his insides.

He stared at the two of them, Darci's blond head bent toward Mandy's darker one. And he knew, without a doubt, that the time had come for him to leave.

Darci tucked a blanket around Mandy's chin, stroked the little girl's hair and came over to stand beside him. The silence stretched between them. When Darci turned to him, the anguish in her eyes hit him in the gut like a runaway bull.

"I could love her, Cole. I could raise her as if she were my own daughter." Her soft voice carried a faint waver. "I think it's best that you leave soon, before I do something stupid again—before I let myself care about her too much."

He wanted to protest, to ask her to let them stay, in spite of his own conclusions. Instead, he nodded as her words pierced his heart. He'd finally found a home, a place where he could love and laugh, but he didn't dare take it. He would only destroy Darci the way he had everyone else in his life. He only hoped he was leaving her soon enough so she could still pick up the pieces and save what was left.

He stroked her cheek, swallowing all the words he wanted to say. "Mandy needs time to heal. The place we're going will expose her to lots of fresh air and horses. She loves horses, wants to ride in the rodeo someday like her daddy did. I'm hoping that will give her the incentive she needs to walk without crutches again."

"Will you be okay?"

Cole almost smiled, but he was afraid his lips would shatter with the effort. Trust Darci to be worried about him when she didn't have a lot going for her, either, at the moment. He wanted to stay, to help her pick up the pieces, but didn't dare. It was already too late for him. He cared for Darci, deeply, but didn't dare let himself admit his love for her. To love her would be to destroy some part of her. Now he had to think of Mandy, had to leave before his little girl was hurt again.

"We'll manage. Do you want to take care of the annulment or should I?"

Her eyes flickered with an emotion he was all too familiar with. After less than a week of pretend marital bliss, it was painful to end a relationship, even though it was something they'd always planned on doing. There was still a sense of loss, a feeling of failure—both sensations were Cole's intimate companions.

"I'll do it. I need to see my lawyer about several other matters, anyway." Her fingers caressed his forearm. "Be happy, Cole. Find someone to love you, someone to give Mandy her dreams."

Her voice cracked on the last sentence, and Cole felt another sharp stab of guilt. In his greed to not share his daughter, he'd forgotten how badly Darci wanted family. And he'd forgotten her need to take care of the wounded. Mandy was silently crying out for the very thing Darci was aching to give.

"I think I'll give up on love. All my attention needs to be focused on raising Mandy."

"You need love. You deserve it, Cole. Don't close that door on yourself."

"I've hurt everyone I've ever loved." All the ghosts from his past rose up to haunt him, to torment him.

"You credit yourself with an awful lot of power over the realities of life."

"It must be true. My mother died while I was young, my father had more important things to do than to love me, my wife was killed and my daughter crippled. Even you haven't escaped unscathed. I've cost you your career, your legacy."

"It would have happened, anyway. Your showing up just hurried along the inevitable. What happened to me wasn't your fault, Cole."

He desperately wanted to believe her, but the evidence proved her wrong. One last time, he allowed himself to touch her, to savor her soft skin. "Didn't your mama ever tell you cowboys will break your heart?" He settled his hand on her shoulder, sadness reflected in his eyes. "Marry a doctor or a lawyer, someone who will take care of you. Not a man like me who'll just walk away when the going gets rough."

She started to protest, but he laid his finger across her lips. He couldn't argue with her anymore or he'd give in to the needs carving up his insides. Because he wanted to stay, to surrender to the temptation to try once more. He just didn't dare.

"Cole, at least spend tonight. You can still leave in the morning."

He was tempted, so tempted he ached with longing. "I can't." His voice broke over the words, and he resisted the urge to call them back. He tried not to see the hurt in her eyes, the yearning.

Turning away from Darci to scoop Mandy into his arms seemed like the hardest thing he'd ever done.

Chapter Ten

The first emotion to really sink through the fog surrounding her was fear. A mind-numbing fear that she'd live the remainder of her life alone, pining for a man who didn't want her. With no chance of love and no chance of the family she'd always dreamed of, the next fifty years or so seemed pretty bleak.

Close on the heels of the fear was anger—a blazing emotion that cost her two broken glasses and a pillow that she beat the stuffing out of. When her energy was exhausted, she sat down among the settling feathers and forced herself to think.

It was quite an endeavor after a week of mindless nothingness.

She had honestly thought losing the presidency of Blackmore's would be the end of her world. She'd been very, very wrong. Cole was her world, the only person who really mattered anymore. Cole and his delightful daughter, a little girl desperately looking for the love that Darci knew she could provide.

Darci had finally realized that she was pouring all her love into a cold, heartless company, expecting it to love and nurture her in return. She'd been using Blackmore's to give her a sense of belonging, using it as a substitute family. But now she could see that only the right man could give her what she wanted, what she needed. And that man was Cole Blackmore.

Jeffrey was little more than a distant memory—a painful one, but so far in the past she barely gave him a moment of her time. What she'd had with Jeffrey had little to do with love, even less to do with passion.

Passion was what she'd experienced in Cole's arms; love was what she felt even after he'd deserted her. He thought he was protecting her, saving her from a terrible disaster—which was the proof she needed to know that he loved her, even if he wouldn't admit it.

What the man didn't realize was that losing him was the worst thing that had ever happened to her, that being without him was slowly destroying her. Blackmore's Gourmet Chocolates barely entered her thoughts anymore.

Without Cole, she knew she would never find love again. And without that love, she could never have the family she'd always dreamed of.

Without Cole, there was nothing.

So what was she going to do about it?

Darci tucked the deflated pillow into her arms and stared out the picture window framing the Rocky Mountains. Scruffy crept closer, gingerly curling into Darci's lap now that her anger was spent. As the minutes ticked into hours, Darci slowly formed a plan of action. Never before had she allowed life to foil her. She'd always found a way around every problem presented to her. And she could do it again.

An idea began to blossom, and a slow smile curved Darci's lips.

First, she had to regain control of Blackmore's. Cole would have nothing to do with her until he had a way to support them, she knew that. The dividend checks they both received were not enough to start a new life, and if her mother had her way, they would be coming to an end soon.

To carry out the first part of her plan, she'd need money. And she knew of only one person who had more money than he knew what to do with. And unlike Cole, Darci wasn't too proud to ask for help when she needed it the most. Todd Perkins would be the target of her first assault.

Now, if she just knew how to get ahold of the old cowboy.

With a flash of inspiration, she grabbed the phone and dialed the offices of Blackmore's Gourmet Chocolates. Todd had left some information with Alex when he'd left, demanding to be notified of the outcome of the board meeting. But Darci had forgotten all about it when Cole had left. When she was finally connected with her former secretary, she was almost shaking with suppressed excitement.

It was going to work, it had to work. Her future depended on it.

"Alex, it's Darci."

A heavy sigh greeted her. "I hope you're planning on regaining control of this company soon. That man is about to drive me crazy with his demands, and he has no clue as to how to run a business."

Darci couldn't help the laughter that bubbled through her. "Well, if you're willing to be a traitor to Jeffrey and the current administration, I could use some help in setting up a coup."

Alex's voice dropped to a conspiratorial undertone. "Anything. Just name it."

"First of all, I need Todd Perkins's address, phone number or some point of contact. I have a business proposition for him. Then, I need to ask you to keep quiet about what you think I'm doing."

"Todd just called this morning to leave the phone number of a hotel he was staying at for a few more days. He had some crazy idea that you might want to talk with him. I know I wrote it down here somewhere."

The sound of rustling papers carried over the phone, and Darci waited impatiently. The energy pulsing through her demanded action, and she was having a difficult time forcing herself to proceed calmly, slowly and methodically. She didn't want to make any mistakes now. Too much hinged on the results.

"Ah, here it is." Alex recited the phone number. "If there's anything else, Darci. Anything."

"Just keep Jeffrey from destroying the place before I can get him out of there. Thanks, Alex. I owe you."

"Hurry, before I take care of the man myself."

Darci smiled at Alex's threat, then hung up and dialed the hotel where Todd was staying. When he finally came on the line, she couldn't resist teasing him a little.

"Here I thought you only slept in the back of that pickup truck of yours. What are you doing in such a fancy place?"

"Well, little gal, every once in a while, I need a good bed, a good meal and a little pampering. This was one of those times." He paused for a breath. "Now, tell me what you're going to do about those varmints that took over your company. What do you need from me?"

The man certainly wasn't the type to waste words on pleasantries. "Money and lots of advice."

"I've got plenty of both. Where do you want to meet?"

"Todd, are you certain? I know I'm imposing..."

"Girl, I owe Cole a lot. He's been there for me whenever I needed him, and I like to think of him as my adopted son. You're his wife so that makes you family. And I stand behind my family. Now quit putting me off. Where do you want to meet?"

Darci kicked her heels off and collapsed on the couch. After an endless round of planning, of lengthy meetings and detailed negotiations, she'd done it. With a loan from Todd, she'd bought up Uncle John's shares of stock in Blackmore's. And Uncle John had been more than happy to take his money and escape from the escalating family tensions.

With the extra votes the purchase had given her, she'd had the power to force out the old board of directors. Within two days, there was a new board in place who shared some of her visions for the future, who would allow Blackmore's Gourmet Chocolates to move forward instead of wallow in the past. A special board meeting was set up for tomorrow, and she was determined to bring to the table another vote on the position of president.

She prowled the condo restlessly. It all hinged on to-morrow. If she couldn't offer Cole some sort of future, she was fairly certain he'd refuse to take her seriously. His damnable pride would keep him from loving her; his fears wouldn't allow him to take a chance.

When she finally crawled out of bed in the morning, she dressed carefully. Makeup once again covered the dark circles under her eyes, and she smiled ruefully when she realized how much of a habit it had become to op-erate on very little sleep. With Cole by her side again, she hoped that would end.

The meeting went well, the new board of directors voted Jeffrey out, and Darci in. After a howl of protest, Jeffrey and Anita left the boardroom, probably to be-gin another round of plotting against her. But Darci knew she was in a much stronger position now. And the successful expansion she envisioned would strengthen her position with the board even further.

Nameplate in hand, she sailed back into her office, threw Jeffrey's nameplate into the wastebasket, and be-gan to clear his files from the desk.

Alex came in behind her, a big smile on his face. "Welcome back. Does this mean I should cancel the new furniture Jeffrey ordered?"

Darci winced. "The company's on the verge of bank-ruptcy and he orders furniture. Makes perfect sense to me. Yes, cancel it. I've always liked what was here." She stroked her fingers across the heavy oak desk her step-father had used and knew a deep sense of pride. She was being given another chance.

Todd opened the door and grinned at her. "Congrat-ulations, honey. I knew you could do it."

She crossed the room and pulled the old cowboy into her arms. "I couldn't have done it without you, Todd. I can't begin to thank you for what you've done."

Todd squirmed, blushed and pulled away. The shuffle of his feet and his downcast eyes clearly said, Aw, shucks, ma'am.

"Now, I need one more favor. Where's Cole?"

He pulled away from her. "I promised him I wouldn't tell you."

Darci stared at him in disbelief. "You mean to say that after all this, all your help, you won't let me go see him?" She threw up her hands and spun away from him. "Why, Todd? What was it all for if not to help Cole?"

Todd's eyes twinkled with mischief. "I said I couldn't tell you. But I think maybe that secretary of yours has some information you might find helpful." He kissed her lightly on the cheek. "Good luck, little gal. You're going to need it. That's one stubborn man you've got yourself, and he isn't going to make it easy for you."

"Maybe he's forgotten just how stubborn I can be when I'm riled. Thanks for your help, Todd. I'd tell you I'll invite you to the wedding, but it's too late for that. Maybe we'll finally have a reception. And you'll be the first to get an invitation."

The excitement that had carried her through these past few weeks faded at the sight of Cole. Now that she was so close to her goal, the fear returned, almost paralyzing her. She'd laid it all on the line for love. But Cole carried some very deep scars. She had to convince him to take a chance, to live his life again, to live it with her. A silent prayer slipped through her, asking for the right words, the right magic, to make him understand.

She leaned against the fence, watching him ride the horse in the corral. A wince marked his handsome face, and she knew that his hip was bothering him. She also knew he was determined to work again, determined to ride again, no matter the cost. His body would never withstand the demands of rodeo, but he could still work as a cowboy on a ranch somewhere.

But if Darci had her way, he'd be working by her side at Blackmore's, and they'd save up enough money to buy a little ranch of their own. A place where their love could flourish and their children could roam free. A place where Cole could still feel the freedom a cowboy's heart demanded.

When he spotted her, he halted the horse, just staring at her as if she were a blurred mirage. Slowly he swung free of the saddle and led the horse into the barn. When he didn't come out, Darci felt her anger simmer to the surface of her emotions. He wouldn't dare to simply ignore her. Then she remembered the night he'd dared try to buy her out when he had no money, and she knew he'd dare anything.

She hadn't driven all this way for nothing. Crossing the mountains to the western slope of Colorado had taken almost all her courage. The hours had been spent trying to shore up her flagging determination until she'd finally reached Todd's ranch.

When Cole didn't return, she started to climb the fence, then forced herself to stop. He had hundreds of acres to move around on. Unless she made him come to her, the battle was lost before the first shot was even fired. She picked up a rock and hefted it in her hand. An overhand pitch landed it against the side of the barn.

A horse whinnied and Darci heard a low curse. She picked up another rock and sent it flying. The third missile was in her hand when he appeared in the doorway. After a slight hesitation, he started toward her.

The faded blue jeans clung to his hips and thighs, reminding her of the few times she'd been pressed against his lean length. Little puffs of dust were kicked up by his boots as each step brought him closer to her. The dusty black hat shadowed his face, but she thought she caught a flicker of longing in the gray depths of his gaze. Leaning her arms against the fence rail, she waited as he walked toward her, enjoying the view Cole presented.

The afternoon sun beat between them, but Darci barely noticed the sweat trickling down her back. As he drew closer, her heart raced with fear and hope. She was laying it all on the line. If she was wrong, even the victory at Blackmore's wouldn't matter.

She wanted Cole in her life until they were both old and gray.

She wanted to watch Mandy grow up, and she wanted to provide the little girl with brothers and sisters.

And she wanted to make love with Cole; she wanted to spend endless nights with her husband at her side.

"What the devil do you think you're doing?"

His deep voice washed over her, and her mind flicked back to the night he'd first appeared in her office. The uncertainty was still there, the slight hesitation, as if he didn't know quite what to expect. Resisting the urge to fling her arms around his neck and show him why she was here, she smiled in greeting.

"I needed to get your attention."

He blinked a few times, then gave a reluctant smile. "What brings you over to the western slope?"

He pushed his hat back, and she was able to see the exhaustion reflected on his face. Her hand twitched with the need to reach out and smooth away the lines of worry. Not now, not yet. Not until he agreed to her crazy plan.

"I suppose you brought some papers for me to sign?"

"Not exactly." The words she wanted to say seemed to be stuck in her throat.

He frowned. "You've filed for the annulment?"

"Not exactly."

His breath came out in a rush. "Why are you here? What's going on, Darci?"

It was now or never. Sucking in a deep breath, she let the words fall from her lips in a tumbling rush. "Cole, I love you. I don't want to end our marriage. I want to stay married, make ours a real marriage. I want to help you raise Mandy."

The silence was thick, unforgiving. He stared at her, no expression on his face, the granite hardness of his jaw unrelenting.

"I can't love you, Darci. I've already explained why."

"And I think you've been hanging around the rodeo too long. You, cowboy, are full of bull."

His lips twitched, but he still glared at her.

Her anger at his stubbornness boiled over. "Damn you, Cole Blackmore. How dare you waltz into my life, make me love you, and then leave without any thought for my feelings? What makes you think you know what's best for me? What makes you so omniscient that you can predict what will happen to me, to us?"

Her anger continued to simmer, and she struggled for the words to express it. "I want it all, Cole, the love, the laughter and even the heartbreak. I want to take the chances, live the risks. Without any risk, life isn't worth living. And I want to take those risks with you. What gives you the right to deny me that chance?"

"Are you finished?" One of his black eyebrows was raised, and there was a gleam of something she couldn't define in his eyes.

"No. I demand we make this a real marriage or I'll sue you for breach of promise."

"Does that law still exist?"

"I don't know, but if it doesn't, I'll find something else to sue you for." She planted her hands on her hips. "Now, are you coming back to Denver or do I have to move over here?"

"Do you intend to run Blackmore's long distance?"

"How did you know about that?"

"You didn't think Todd would tell me, did you." He waited for her response. When there wasn't one, he continued. "I intend to earn my keep, Darci. I won't let you support me, and I can't just live off my dividend checks. I need to work."

"I'll give you the damn company to run. I don't want it, I only want you. And Mandy." She scuffed the toe of her tennis shoe in the dirt. "You're evading my questions. What do you intend to do about our marriage?"

With a lithe grace that had always fascinated her, he braced his arm on the top rail and vaulted over the fence. His feet had barely touched the ground before he pulled her into his arms. His mouth swooped down to cover hers, and she groaned at his touch.

Opening her mouth, she invited him inside, teasing his tongue with hers. Angling her head, she pulled him closer, relishing the tightening in his body. Heat exploded deep inside her, setting off a chain of longing she struggled to control. His hat fell to the ground when she combed her fingers through his hair, but he didn't seem to notice.

When they finally broke apart, they were both breathing hard. Staring at him, she saw the need, the longing, reflected in his eyes. "Is that a yes?"

"This has been the longest month of my life. I've almost called you a dozen different times, but when I didn't hear from you, I figured you didn't feel the same way I did."

His callused hands cupped her face, and he looked into her eyes. "This might be totally selfish, but I love you, Darci. I want to be your husband in every sense of the word." He pressed a quick kiss on her lips, then pulled her head against his chest. "But I'm still afraid. There's so much that could go wrong, so many ways I could hurt you."

"We'll face that together, Cole. If we love each other enough, I believe we can overcome anything the world throws our way. We have to try, or we'll be worse off without each other."

"You really believe that?"

"With every fiber of my being."

"Do you believe enough for both of us?"

A sense of power surged through her. "Without a doubt."

"Then I guess it's settled." He glanced toward the house. "When can we start the honeymoon?"

Her fingers traced a path across his chest, dropping lower with each sweep. "Now?"

He caught her questing fingers with a gruff laugh. "I've...we've got a daughter wandering around here somewhere. Maybe we'd better wait until tonight."

He kissed her again, lingering over the taste, the texture of her lips. His heart flowed with the love he'd denied for too long. He finally had a true sense of coming home, and it had nothing to do with a fancy house or a sprawling ranch.

"Let's go home." He whispered the words against her lips, stealing another kiss before letting her answer.

"And where would that be?"

"Wherever you are, honey. Wherever you and my family are, that's my home."

Epilogue

The young girl guided the horse around the barrels, determination in every movement. Cole stood with his arm around Darci's waist, fighting the tears that threatened to fill his eyes. "I never thought I'd see this day."

Darci squeezed his hand in her excitement. "She's good, Cole. Really good. I think it's time to look into a better horse for her."

Cole frowned, the old fears still hovering too close to the surface of his thoughts. "I don't know if I'm ready for that."

Darci framed his face with her hands, pulling his head close enough to press a kiss on his lips. "Let her go, Cole. The doctor said she was completely healed, that she's just like any other young lady who will get all the bumps and bruises of growing up. Let her live her life the way she needs to. What happens, happens, and we'll deal with it then. We'll deal with it together."

"But Mandy hasn't been walking that long. I thought I was being the ultimate parent by letting her ride. And barrel racing was another major step forward."

"She'll be fine. We'll be fine. Let her grow."

Cole sighed, knowing that once again, his wife was right. He couldn't wrap Mandy up in cotton and keep her safe any more than he could Darci. It was hard letting go, letting life happen, but he was learning.

The mailman pulled up, disrupting their discussion. "Just one letter today, Mrs. Blackmore. See ya tomorrow."

Darci took the envelope, turning it over to view the return address. "It's from my mother."

Cole pulled her closer. "Do you want me to open it?" He couldn't resist the urge to protect her from at least this. They'd had no communication with Anita Blackmore for six months, but he knew how the woman could hurt Darci with just a few choice words.

Darci sighed. "No, she's my mother." Hesitating, she finally tore open the seal and pulled out an ornate card. "Oh, my."

"What?"

"It's a wedding card, congratulating us on our marriage. Cole, I think she's finally accepted us, accepted everything that's happened. This is her way of making an apology."

Planting a kiss on her lips, Cole resisted the urge to carry his wife into the house. "I love you, honey."

"Good." She wrapped her arms around his neck. "Will you still love me when I'm fat?"

His hand traced over her slim hips as he raised one eyebrow, an unexplained excitement flaring through him. "Care to explain that comment?"

"In about seven-and-a-half months, I'll be elephant-size. Will you still love me then?"

Fire lit the love smoldering inside him. "You won't get rid of me that easily. I'll love you forever."

She reached up for another kiss, whispering sweet words against his lips. "Little girls' dreams really do come true."

*   *   *   *   *

The first book in the exciting new
Fortune's Children series is
HIRED HUSBAND
by *New York Times* bestselling writer
Rebecca Brandewyne

Beginning in July 1996
Only from Silhouette Books

Here's an exciting sneak preview....

Minneapolis, Minnesota

As Caroline Fortune wheeled her dark blue Volvo into
the underground parking lot of the towering, glass-and-
steel structure that housed the global headquarters of
Fortune Cosmetics, she glanced anxiously at her gold
Piaget wristwatch. An accident on the snowy freeway
had caused rush-hour traffic to be a nightmare this
morning. As a result, she was running late for her
9:00 a.m. meeting—and if there was one thing her
grandmother, Kate Winfield Fortune, simply couldn't
abide, it was slack, unprofessional behavior on the job.
And lateness was the sign of a sloppy, disorganized
schedule.

Involuntarily, Caroline shuddered at the thought of
her grandmother's infamous wrath being unleashed
upon her. The stern rebuke would be precise, apropos,
scathing and delivered with coolly raised, condemna-
tory eyebrows and in icy tones of haughty grandeur that
had in the past reduced many an executive—even the
male ones—at Fortune Cosmetics not only to obsequi-
ous apologies, but even to tears. Caroline had seen it
happen on more than one occasion, although, much to
her gratitude and relief, she herself was seldom a target
of her grandmother's anger. And she wouldn't be this

morning, either, not if she could help it. That would be a disastrous way to start out the new year.

Grabbing her Louis Vuitton totebag and her black leather portfolio from the front passenger seat, Caroline stepped gracefully from the Volvo and slammed the door. The heels of her Maud Frizon pumps clicked briskly on the concrete floor as she hurried toward the bank of elevators that would take her up into the skyscraper owned by her family. As the elevator doors slid open, she rushed down the long, plushly carpeted corridors of one of the hushed upper floors toward the conference room.

By now Caroline had her portfolio open and was leafing through it as she hastened along, reviewing her notes she had prepared for her presentation. So she didn't see Dr. Nicolai Valkov until she literally ran right into him. Like her, he had his head bent over his own portfolio, not watching where he was going. As the two of them collided, both their portfolios and the papers inside went flying. At the unexpected impact, Caroline lost her balance, stumbled, and would have fallen had not Nick's strong, sure hands abruptly shot out, grabbing hold of her and pulling her to him to steady her. She gasped, startled and stricken, as she came up hard against his broad chest, lean hips and corded thighs, her face just inches from his own—as though they were lovers about to kiss.

Caroline had never been so close to Nick Valkov before, and, in that instant, she was acutely aware of him—not just as a fellow employee of Fortune Cosmetics but also as a man. Of how tall and ruggedly handsome he was, dressed in an elegant, pin-striped black suit cut in the European fashion, a crisp white shirt, a foulard tie and a pair of Cole Haan loafers. Of how dark his thick, glossy hair and his deep-set eyes framed by raven-wing brows were—so dark that they were almost black, despite the bright, fluorescent lights that blazed overhead. Of the whiteness of his straight teeth against his bronzed skin as a brazen, mocking grin slowly curved his wide, sensual mouth.

"Actually, I *was* hoping for a sweet roll this morning—but I daresay you would prove even tastier, Ms. Fortune," Nick drawled impertinently, his low, silky voice tinged with a faint accent born of the fact that Russian, not English, was his native language.

At his words, Caroline flushed painfully, embarrassed and annoyed. If there was one person she always attempted to avoid at Fortune Cosmetics, it was Nick Valkov. Following the breakup of the Soviet Union, he had emigrated to the United States, where her grandmother had hired him to direct the company's research and development department. Since that time, Nick had constantly demonstrated marked, traditional, Old World tendencies that had led Caroline to believe he not only had no use for equal rights but also would actually have been more than happy to turn back the clock several centuries where females were concerned. She thought his remark was typical of his attitude toward women: insolent, arrogant and domineering. Really, the man was simply insufferable!

Caroline couldn't imagine what had ever prompted her grandmother to hire him—and at a highly generous salary, too—except that Nick Valkov was considered one of the foremost chemists anywhere on the planet. Deep down inside Caroline knew that no matter how he behaved, Fortune Cosmetics was extremely lucky to have him. Still, that didn't give him the right to manhandle and insult her!

"I assure you that you would find me more bitter than a cup of the strongest black coffee, Dr. Valkov," she insisted, attempting without success to free her trembling body from his steely grip, while he continued to hold her so near that she could feel his heart beating steadily in his chest—and knew he must be equally able to feel the erratic hammering of her own.

"Oh, I'm willing to wager there's more sugar and cream to you than you let on, Ms. Fortune." To her utter mortification and outrage, she felt one of Nick's hands slide insidiously up her back and nape to her luxuriant mass of sable hair, done up in a stylish French twist.

"You know so much about fashion," he murmured, eyeing her assessingly, pointedly ignoring her indignation and efforts to escape from him. "So why do you always wear your hair like this...so tightly wrapped and severe? I've never seen it down. Still, that's the way it needs to be worn, you know...soft, loose, tangled about your face. As it is, your hair fairly cries out for a man to take the pins from it, so he can see how long it is. Does it fall past your shoulders?" He quirked one eyebrow inquisitively, a mocking half smile still twisting his lips, letting her know he was enjoying her obvious discomfiture. "You aren't going to tell me, are you? What a pity. Because my guess is that it does—and I'd like to know if I'm right. And these glasses." He indicated the large, square, tortoiseshell frames perched on her slender, classic nose. "I think you use them to hide behind more than you do to see. I'll bet you don't actually even need them at all."

Caroline felt the blush that had yet to leave her cheeks deepen, its heat seeming to spread throughout her entire quivering body. Damn the man! Why must he be so infuriatingly perceptive?

Because everything that Nick suspected was true.

*   *   *   *   *

To read more, don't miss
HIRED HUSBAND
by Rebecca Brandewyne,
Book One in the new
FORTUNE'S CHILDREN series,
beginning this month and available only from
Silhouette Books!

New York Times Bestselling Author
REBECCA BRANDEWYNE

Launches a new twelve-book series—FORTUNE'S CHILDREN
beginning in July 1996 with Book One

Hired Husband

Caroline Fortune knew her marriage to Nick Valkov was in
name only. She would help save the family business, Nick
would get a green card, and a paper marriage would suit both
of them. Until Caroline could no longer deny the feelings Nick
stirred in her and the practical union turned passionate.

MEET THE FORTUNES—a family whose legacy is greater than
riches. Because where there's a will…there's a wedding!

Look for Book Two, *The Millionaire and the Cowgirl*,
by Lisa Jackson. Available in August 1996 wherever Silhouette
books are sold.

MILLION DOLLAR SWEEPSTAKES

Who can resist a Texan...or a Calloway?

This September, award-winning author
ANNETTE BROADRICK
returns to Texas, with a brand-new
story about the Calloways...

SONS
→OF←
TEXAS
Rogues and Ranchers

CLINT: The brave leader. Used to keeping secrets.

CADE: The Lone Star Stud. Used to having women
fall at his feet...

MATT: The family guardian. Used to handling
trouble...

They must discover the identity of the mystery
woman with Calloway eyes—and uncover a
conspiracy that threatens their family....

Look for **SONS OF TEXAS:** Rogues and Ranchers
in September 1996!

Only from Silhouette...where passion lives.

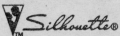

Silhouette's recipe for a sizzling summer:

* Take the best-looking cowboy in South Dakota
* Mix in a brilliant bachelor
* Add a sexy, mysterious sheikh
* Combine their stories into one collection and you've got one sensational super-hot read!

Summer Sizzlers

MEN OF *Summer*

Three short stories by these favorite authors:

Kathleen Eagle
Joan Hohl
Barbara Faith

Available this July wherever Silhouette books are sold.

Look us up on-line at: http://www.romance.net

Silhouette®
™

SS96

You're About to Become a Privileged Woman

Reap the rewards of fabulous free gifts and benefits with proofs-of-purchase from Silhouette and Harlequin books

Pages & Privileges™

It's our way of thanking you for buying our books at your favorite retail stores.

Harlequin and Silhouette— the most privileged readers in the world!

For more information about Harlequin and Silhouette's PAGES & PRIVILEGES program call the Pages & Privileges Benefits Desk: 1-503-794-2499

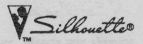

Silhouette®

SR-PP155